THE HIDEAWAY

PAVILION

Praise for Thornhill *by Pam Smy*

'Beautiful, moody, sad, and spooky—all at once.'
Kirkus Starred Review (US)

'. . . an unsettling, deeply memorable read.'
Guardian

'Brilliant'
Vivian French

'Smy uses this hybrid format to weave
a chilling tale that highlights the importance
of kindness and child advocacy while emphasizing
the lasting damage wrought by abuse and neglect.'
Publishers Weekly (US)

'. . . an ambitious and beguiling tale . . .'
The Bookseller

THE HIDEAWAY

PAM SMY

PAVILION

First published in the UK in 2021 by
Pavilion Books Company Limited
43 Great Ormond Street
London, WC1N 3HZ

The poem 'All Souls' Night' © The Literary Executors of Frances Cornford (1886-1960)

Publisher: Neil Dunnicliffe
Editor: Alice Corrie
Art Director: Ness Wood

ISBN: 9781843654797

A CIP catalogue record for this book is available from the British Library.

10 9 8 7 6 5 4 3 2 1

Reproduction by Mission, Hong Kong
Printed by 1010 Printing International Ltd, China

This book can be ordered at
www.pavilionbooks.com,
or try your local bookshop.

MIX
Paper from
responsible sources
FSC
www.fsc.org
FSC® C016973

For those who long to be reunited with those they have lost

Chapter One

30th October, 24 Brownsfield Close, 8 p.m.

Billy tried to slide the drawer shut as quietly as he could. He folded a couple of hoodies and stuffed them into the bag with his joggers, jeans, socks and pants. He slid some cash into his back pocket.

He could hear the familiar noises from downstairs. It was starting again and he knew it would follow the same pattern.

I'm sorry, Jeff, I didn't mean . . .

He packed a pen and a few books.

Please, Jeff! It won't happen again . . .

He pulled the sleeping bag from under his bed and squeezed it into a backpack. He grabbed his rolled-up camping mat and strapped it to the bottom of the bag. He took his pillow but not his mobile. Where he was going he wouldn't be able to charge it anyway and he didn't want to be found.

It was just a silly mistake . . .

He slipped the notebook he had been writing in back into its usual place on the bookshelf and made sure it couldn't be seen.

Then Jeff's gruff growl of a voice started just as he knew it would.

You stupid cow!

Billy pulled the backpack closed, zipped up his bag and put his coat on. He took one final look at his room. Was it tidy enough? He always tried to keep it tidy, just to help his mum out. He tiptoed down the stairs, although Jeff was shouting now, so they wouldn't hear him anyway. As he crept along the hall he saw, through the frosted glass of the sitting-room door, Jeff's silhouette looming over his mum.

I just don't know what to do! You never listen! You drive me bloody crazy, woman! You make me . . .

In the kitchen Billy quietly pulled open the cutlery drawer. He took a spoon, fork and knife, and after hesitating for a few seconds he decided to also take all the sharp chopping knives. He wrapped them in a tea towel. Then he took string, candles, matches, a torch and a roll of bin bags from under the sink. He dropped some apples, cheese and half the loaf of bread into a bag. As he turned the key in the lock of the back door, click, he heard the first . . .

Slap!

Even though he had heard it hundreds of times before, the shock of it made him wince, but, determined to follow his plan, he stepped out into the cold of the night and shut the door on the sound of his mum crying.

CHAPTER TWO

A fierce wind battered the rain hard against pavements and windows. Despite having his hood up, rain splattered on to his forehead and into his eyes, running in rivulets down his jacket as he walked purposefully through the streets. He followed the route he had rehearsed in his mind so many times before. Passers-by tucked their heads deep into their coat collars as they hurried home. Cars splashed through puddles, their headlamps casting blurred beams of light.

No one was going to take any notice of one boy in a hoody with a bag and a backpack. He was just another anonymous shadow slipping past them on the dark, wet street.

In fact, not one person that night would recall seeing Billy at all.

He kept his head down as he walked past the houses he passed each day on his way to school. Then he turned out across the rec and slipped down a few back alleys to make sure no one saw him and then out to where the houses became bigger and further apart, set back from the road, surrounded by trees and well-groomed gardens. Warm yellow light glowed from the windows, illuminating cosy scenes of families watching TV or eating dinner together.

He walked until he found the gap between two houses. It was a wide path, its entrance almost hidden by bushes. Taking his torch from his backpack, he shone it around him.

LANE

Was it the right place? The torchlight picked out the sign behind the clump of nettles. ALL SOULS' LANE. *This was it.*

The lane was unlit and very quiet. Away from the road, the houses and the street lamps, the night seemed to become darker and the sound of his footsteps louder. On he walked, his torchlight picking out the scattering of leaves as the wind blew around him. On and on into the leafy black and the gate at the end of the lane.

That was where he stopped.

This was where he wanted to be.

This was where he knew he wouldn't be found.

He swung open the gate and stepped into the graveyard beyond . . .

CHAPTER THREE

30th October, 26 Brownsfield Close, 8.45 p.m.

Suzie stopped midway through unpacking another box of books, leant across and clicked off the radio.

There it was again.

The noise from next door.

She had only been in Brownsfield Close a few weeks and this was the second time she had heard an argument through the walls.

She stood as still as possible, books in one hand and strained to hear what was happening next door. She couldn't make out the words but she *could* hear the bellow of a man's voice and the occasional crash of . . . what? Crockery? She wasn't sure.

It went quiet. She held her breath, trying to imagine what had happened. All couples argued but what she had heard through the wall was unsettling. It was wretched. Desperate. Frightening even. But all couples were different, weren't they? Maybe her new neighbours just had a fiery relationship. How could she tell? And maybe it sounded worse than it really was. She hadn't actually *seen* anything.

Then Suzie heard the man's voice coming from the hall, just a few metres from where she was standing.

She clicked off the light and walked through to the sitting-room window.

The door of number 24 slammed shut and the man pulled on a jacket, pausing at the end of the garden. Suzie watched as he turned away from the bluster of the wind and clicked at a lighter. His face was temporarily lit by the small flame and then it was gone. Only the orange tip of the cigarette was visible against his dark shape. He blew out a long breath of smoke, stepped out on to the pavement and walked away into the night.

Chapter Four

Twists of ivy snaked round tree trunks and seeped over gravestones. Dark rows of yews lined an overgrown path, their swaying, shifting branches forming a tunnel that Billy lit up with the weak beam of his torch. Branches, graves and statues flashed in and out of sight in the torchlight. Billy swung the beam to the centre of the graveyard where, in the middle of it all, stood an old stone chapel. It was a small, squat, dark shape against the night sky and was dwarfed by the trees around it.

Everything was so different in the dark. He had known it would be but hadn't imagined it like this . . . So inky-black and so lonely.

He shivered as the rain ran down his neck. He felt small

and lost. But anything was better than being at home. Even this.

Hesitantly he took the path between the yews, his torch lighting the carved headstones that lined the graveyard. He tried to make out the exact path but the tangle of weeds obscured the way and snatched at his ankles. He dragged his wet jeans through the leaves, snapping twigs underfoot and swivelling the torchlight between what was at his feet and the direction the pathway took ahead. The wind swished through the trees and his torch beam lit up spindly branches as they danced across his path, catching at his jacket and snagging on his hood like brittle fingers reaching for him.

He stopped, confused about where he was. Had he gone the wrong way? Everything looked so different in the dark. He gripped the torch and swung it around him. The hairs on the back of his neck stood up. His heart thumped.

Don't bottle it now, he told himself. *Keep going. You can't go back.*

Then he spotted the wall again. All he needed to do now was to follow the outline of the graveyard and he'd find

what he was looking for. *Surely it was along here somewhere?*
He stumbled forward over roots and pushed aside the wet
stray branches that brushed against his face. Then the beam
of light from his torch picked out the first of the row of trees
marking the edge of the graveyard. *At last!* Between their
closely spaced trunks he traced the shape of the hedges
beyond, until he spotted the dark-domed mound of ivy that
he'd been searching for.

This was it!

In his relief he staggered forward, almost into a run, his
backpack bumping, the other bag banging against his calves,
the torch beam jolting up and down.

He was nearly there.

Nearly safe.

Then, in his hurry, he tripped and tumbled face first on
to the path.

The torch spun away.

The light flickered and went out.

His cheekbone scraped some bark.

His bag burst open and spilled its contents all around him on the path.

Billy lay there a moment in the dark. Splayed out. Panting. Panic rose in his chest. His head hurt. He had dirt in his mouth and he could taste blood on his lips. The rain splattered on his hood and water ran between his fingers.

He staggered to his feet and cast about him for his stuff – the bread and apples and bin bags. The torch was gone. It took a while to adjust to the darkness but

gradually he could make out the shape of the tree trunks at the edge of the graveyard and the mound of ivy, as big as a garden shed, beyond. Clutching his belongings to his chest he took one cautious shuffling step after another until he made it through the gap in the trees.

He needed to work fast. The rain was icy cold. His teeth were chattering and his body shivering all over. When he had planned this moment he hadn't imagined it would be this dark and this wet and that he would be *this* scared. Trees swayed above his head, sending swirls of autumn leaves over the graveyard as he made a pile of his stuff and then, with both hands, he plunged forward and rummaged through the wet ivy.

He felt concrete beneath the undergrowth. This was it! Then he traced the circular wall with his hands until he found an opening. He tugged and tugged at the twist of leaves until it came away from the concrete blocks like a curtain. Then he reached back for his bag and threw it through the opening. He took off his backpack and rolled that in too. Then, sliding sideways under the ivy and stepping down, he was inside. At last!

He had first noticed the pillbox on a school history trip to the graveyard nearly a year ago. Mr Jeffries had been talking about the casualties of the First World War, pointing out gravestones dedicated to those who had died in battle, many less than ten years older than Billy and his classmates. Billy had hung at the back, distancing himself from James Johnson and Max Hilliard who were, as usual, larking about. He was only half listening when he had spotted the ivy between the trees with the glimpse of a building beneath. It was a Second World War pillbox, a tiny hut, built from concrete blocks as part of the country's defence in case of attack. It was there and then, in that history lesson, with Mr Jeffries droning on in the background, that Billy had realized he had found the perfect hiding place should he ever need it.

And tonight he needed it.

It was even darker inside. Unable to see, Billy fumbled with numb fingers at the zip on his backpack and reached into an inside pocket for his bike light. He clicked it on and looked around.

The floor was compacted dirt and was covered with leaves and the odd crisp packet and cigarette butt. He scrabbled around, scraping the rubbish aside, unrolled some bin bags and laid them out like a bed. He flattened out his camping mat. Then unpacked his sleeping bag and rolled it out with shaking hands and he put his pillow in place.

He pulled out some candles and matches. It took several attempts to strike a light. Eventually the candles were lit. He dug them into the dirt floor so they balanced there, the light flickering around the low walls.

Slowly he peeled off his wet trainers and socks and slid out of his cold jeans. He shrugged off the wet hoody and pulled a clean, dry one over his T-shirt. He put on his joggers and then three pairs of socks. He felt the warmth seep into his body, although his teeth were still chattering.

So this is it, he thought. *I've done it.*

He lay there listening to the sounds outside, the thump of his heart steadily slowing as warmth returned to his body. The rain pelted the leaf-covered roof of the pillbox and the wind rushed through the tall branches of the trees above. Somewhere a fox barked.

Billy felt safe here, cocooned in the pillbox in the middle of a graveyard of all places. So much safer than he felt at home. He was relieved he had got away at last, but, as he drifted off to sleep, it was the sound of his mum's crying that filled his head.

Chapter Five

31st October, 24 Brownsfield Close, 2 a.m.

Grace McKenna made herself a cup of tea and carried it through to the sitting room. Curling up on the sofa in the dark, she sat watching the rain outside in the street. Her hands were still shaking and her cheek was throbbing, even though Jeff had long since slammed his way out of the house and staggered back in, drunk, hours later. She could hear his snores vibrating through the house from the room above her.

As she stared out at the houses in her cul-de-sac her mind didn't replay the events of the evening but skimmed across incidents from the past. How did she get here? She looked out at the street. She had lived there for years but she knew no one. There wasn't a single person in that street she could name, let alone pop in and have a chat with. She was utterly friendless and alone, except for Billy, of course. Then she remembered her mother's stony expression when she had told her that she was expecting Billy. And then, many rows and phone calls later, the feeling of collecting her bag of childhood belongings from the doorstep, aware that her mother was watching her, pinch-faced at the net curtains, her timid father hesitating somewhere behind.

She recalled the feeling of holding Billy in her arms for the first time and that flood of love. That instant need to protect him and keep him close.

And those early years of bringing up Billy alone. They were inseparable. So close. But doing everything on her own had been tough. Her friends had slipped away. Her family had disowned her. Other than Billy, she was lonely.

And then she thought about Jeff. How nice he had been. How kind, charming and reassuring. He had said he wanted to look after her and Billy.

If only she knew then what she knew now.

She sipped at her sugary tea, then pulled the blanket from the back of the sofa.

'You made your bed. Now you can lie in it!' her mother had said.

If only she could see me now, Grace thought, as she patted a cushion into place under her head and curled up to sleep.

Chapter Six

When Billy woke the next morning he had never felt so frozen. His jaw ached. His lip throbbed. His feet were numb. And he felt overwhelmed by sadness.

He crawled out of his makeshift bed, stiff with cold.

The sleeping bag was damp under his fingers and covered with a sheen of morning dew. He slipped into his coat and trainers, unzipped the sleeping bag and wrapped it like a cloak round his shoulders. Then he stepped through the curtain of ivy, out of the pillbox, and into the dim morning light.

A swirl of autumnal mist hung low across the ground. Some twisted trees

and taller headstones were visible in the gloom. Yew trees peeped above the grey. But most of the graveyard was hidden. Shrouded in fog. The wind and rain from last night had gone and an eerie stillness had settled around the grave-yard. Other than the sound of his own breathing, all was quiet. He was quite alone. And yet, as he stood staring into the wall of mist, Billy felt as though he was being watched.

The hairs on the back of his neck prickled.

Pull yourself together, McKenna! he thought. *If you can't see anything or anyone, they certainly can't see you. And, remember, no one knows where you are. They probably haven't even noticed you've gone.*

Anyway, he had things to do. Back in the pillbox, Billy pulled a bin bag from his backpack and filled it with the pile of leaves and rubbish from the floor. Tying string to the knotted trunks of ivy and through the tiny windows of the pillbox, he rigged up a washing line across the small circular room, and, unwrapping the sleeping bag from his shoulders, he hung it up away from the damp floor. Then he pulled a chunk off the loaf and took an apple, picked up his rubbish, and stepped back out into the morning air.

It was warmer now and the fog was lifting, although it still clung to pockets of the graveyard, misting up the pathways between gravestones and lurking under the trees.

Steadily he made his way back round the path through the yews. Somewhere near the entrance to the graveyard he was sure there were some bins. Sound was muffled. Damp leaves slid under his trainers. It *was* quiet but Billy couldn't shake off the feeling that he was being watched. A few times he stopped, straining his ears to pick up any sounds other than his own, staring at patches of fog, convinced that there were shadowy shapes shifting under the trees. Only to find, as he edged his way cautiously forward, that there was nothing and nobody there.

Billy clunked the bag of rubbish into the bin and made his way back into the graveyard, munching on bread as he walked. The grass was high and the tops of headstones peeped out above a mess of brambles and nettles.

I guess this is my back garden now. Better get to know the neighbours!

He stopped a few stones in and brushed aside the weeds.

*In Loving Memory of a
Devoted Mother and Grandmother
May Good
1906–1986*

*Albert Ward
So Dearly Loved, so Greatly Missed
1878–1894
And his faithful companion
Rufus*

Ada Cunningham
Died 1969
Aged 87
Also of her husband
Ebenezer Cunningham
Died on 12th February 1977
Aged 95 years

What had Ebenezer's life been like without Ada for those last eight years? Billy wondered.

Many of the gravestones were so covered in ivy that they were unreadable and on several the words had eroded away with time. Only one memorial in the whole graveyard was neat and well looked after. The others were mostly obscured by weeds and nettles. Billy stepped cautiously between the uneven stones, the undergrowth tugging at his legs as he walked.

At Rest
In Loving Memory of a
Dear Husband and Father
William Carter
1902–1945

In Memory of William Wing
1881–1918
His Wife Clara Wing
1884–1918
and their children
Ernest
1903–1904
Arthur
1905–1906
And Stanley, Gilbert, Kathleen and Joyce
Who were all suddenly called away
1918

So many people. The stories of their lives hinted at on these stones but now unseen in the twist and tangle of weeds. Some listed family names – one long life lived after another. Others were the graves of tiny children – 'Our Springtime Baby' or 'Our Cherished Daughter'. In leaving details of their relatives carved into stone, families had also recorded their sense of love and loss – *'Beloved'*, *'Forever missed'* or *'Always in our hearts'*.

The yearning and sorrow of these people was clear for Billy to see. He imagined bustling families gathered round fireplaces. Warm, happy and safe. And he thought back to the very real lives he had glimpsed through the windows of the houses he had passed the night before. To lose someone would leave such a void in those families. Would *he* be missed like this? Would *anyone* notice if he wasn't there?

But what of the lives on the other stones? The ones with just a name and dates?

Winston Cleaver
1895–1918

Marion Bird
Died 3rd December 1970

Who were they? What had their lives been like? Had they died alone? And who grieved for them? Who would remember them?

As he took another bite of bread Billy's mind slid back to his mother.

Chapter Seven

31st October, 24 Brownsfield Close, 9.30 a.m.

Grace woke up to find Jeff crouched beside the sofa, a steaming mug of tea in his hand.

'Morning, sleepyhead. I'm making bacon and eggs. Want some?'

He kissed her forehead and headed back to the kitchen.

Grace slowly rolled her head to ease the stiffness in her neck and tentatively touched her bruised cheek. *Mustn't forget to get some concealer on that*, she thought. Quietly, slowly, she folded the blankets and arranged them neatly on the back of the sofa, trying to gather her thoughts before following Jeff through to the kitchen. She knew she must not mention what had happened last night. She mustn't upset Jeff again. She must behave as if everything was fine and will be fine. She swallowed down the feeling of wanting to cry, took a deep breath and followed the smell of breakfast.

Jeff was clearly trying to make amends just like he always did. To pretend that nothing had happened. The kitchen table was set for two. Jeff whistled as he scraped eggs out of a pan and on to buttered toast. Autumn sunlight streamed through the window. It was a beautiful morning.

'I rang work – said I had a bit of trouble with the van and that I'd be in a bit late,' said Jeff with a smile. 'Thought we could do with a treat.'

'This is lovely. Thank you.'

Grace forced a smile. The skin on her face felt tight.

'Did you see Billy before he left for school? I didn't hear him go,' she asked.

'No. He must have crept out while we were both still asleep.'

'He's a good boy,' said Grace as she pushed bits of egg around her plate, watching as Jeff shovelled forkfuls into his mouth.

He is a good boy, she thought.

He deserves better than this.

CHAPTER EIGHT

It was when Billy reached the stone angel that the ache started. The sun had broken through the yew trees and a ray of light lit the statue. She almost glowed in a halo of golden light as she looked down on him.

The memory flooded back like a sharp pain. His mum. Years ago. A picnic in the park. Her blonde hair lit by the sun as she laughed and laughed, hugging Billy tightly as the ducks pecked at their sandwiches. She laughed all the time back then. Before Jeff. She had been so, so beautiful, and their life had seemed so carefree and happy. Billy adored her.

It had always just been the two of them. Billy didn't have a dad, well, not one he had met anyway. Apparently his dad didn't even know he existed. But Billy knew all about him.

He knew how his mum had fallen in love with his dad the first time she had seen him at sixth-form college. She wanted to attract his attention so she had stayed up night after night knitting him the longest ever scarf. When it was finished she had walked across the canteen with it and given it to him. He had laughed and wrapped it round his neck and for the next six months they were inseparable. Billy knew about his dad's twinkling blue eyes and his beautiful black curly hair. He knew that his dad was shy and sensitive and that he and Billy's mum had a lot in common. They were both from strict families who would have disapproved of them having a serious relationship at their age, so they kept their love a secret – like Romeo and Juliet, his mum said.

But then his dad started hanging out with a group of friends from the other side of town. They lived in big houses and some already had cars. He was impressed by their clothes and their holidays and gradually he started hanging out with them way more than with Grace. She wasn't interested in them at all. When it was just the two of them together everything was perfect, his mum said, but those times became rarer, and his dad seemed to be drifting away from her. It was as if he was under a spell. He talked more and more about wanting to stretch his wings, to leave this 'crummy old town' and see more of the world. He talked enviously about the places his new mates had been to and about his plans to hitch across Europe and explore the world. Grace was more sensible and pointed out that he would need money and places to stay, but he didn't listen. He was determined to go. Billy's mum said that while she spent her time dreaming of the two of them being together, Billy's dad spent his time dreaming of far-flung adventures.

Then one day Billy's dad turned up with a packed bag and a train ticket in his pocket.

He promised that he would be back soon. That he just wanted to see a bit of the world. He told Billy's mum that he loved her with all his heart. And then he was gone.

It was a few weeks later that Billy's mum discovered she was pregnant. She tried to find out where he was but no one seemed to know. She received a few postcards, hastily written, from different parts of the country and then one or two from France, saying that he loved her and missed her and that he would be back soon. But there was never a return address and gradually the cards stopped arriving. By the time her belly was big with Billy she realized she would be on her own. She never got to see his dad again.

So it had always been just the two of them. Billy's mum said it was difficult at first being seventeen and on her own with a baby. She had found it hard seeing her old school friends giggling by the pizzas in the supermarket, or trying on lipsticks in the make-up aisle as they planned nights out and whispered about who they fancied, while Grace shopped for nappies and baby food. But she loved Billy so much that she had made it work.

She had to.

Even though it was just the two of them, his mum sang

and laughed and was rarely cross. She always loved giving him cuddles on the sofa and reading him stories before bed. His beautiful mum whose hair glowed like sunshine.

Their little flat was a nest of books and toys and knitting, blankets and pictures from nursery and school photos on the fridge. It was cluttered and messy but cosy and full of all their favourite things. Billy hadn't realized how happy they had been until, bit by bit, everything began to change.

At first he had liked it when Jeff came round. He was interesting and funny and they all went on trips together and sang in the car and giggled at rude jokes. His mum was happy so Billy was happy.

But then he had to switch schools when they moved in with Jeff and he didn't know anyone. It would have been okay, because he still had his mum, but then Jeff decided that Billy was 'too old' for bedtime stories on the sofa and that he was 'big enough' to manage his homework on his own.

His mum began to fuss over the tidiness of the house – 'Jeff likes it neat, darling; maybe you could keep your Lego upstairs for now?' – and seemed to spend longer wiping and cooking and washing and arranging and rearranging.

She stopped knitting and the balls of coloured wool disappeared from the sitting room.

Little by little their past life was tidied away, as if it had never even existed.

Billy spent more time in his room so as 'not to get under Jeff's feet' and from his room he could hear Jeff complain about this and that, and then, later on, the arguments about this and that, and later still much worse . . .

His mum became tense, anxious. Her smiles were nervous and her eyes didn't sparkle. Billy became quieter – keen not to cause any trouble. In the five years they had been living with Jeff he made sure that he worked hard at school, did his homework, kept his room tidy, got himself ready in the mornings and took himself off to bed every night. He never invited his old friends round, worried about what they might see and hear, and that they, like him, wouldn't recognize this woman with her hair scraped back into a ponytail, dark shadows under her eyes and a nervous twitch to her mouth.

'She's a bit worn down, ain't she?'

Billy jumped out of his skin. Staggering back he found he was no longer alone. By his side stood an old man, his checked shirt rolled up at the sleeves, tanned arms exposed, cap shading his wrinkled eyes, cords tucked into his wellies.

Billy was so confused that for a minute he thought this man must be talking about his mother, until he realized that he was nodding towards the statue.

'She used to be a beauty. The most glorious figure in this whole graveyard.'

The man fumbled in his pocket.

'But, much like the rest of this place, she needs a little bit of love and care.'

The man stared at Billy out of the corner of his eye.

'Shouldn't you be at school, lad?' he asked, passing across a clean hankie.

It was only then that Billy realized that he had been crying. He blushed and wiped at his face but the man carried on.

'Well, I suppose one day off won't hurt, eh? But you don't want to hang around here. And someone will be missing you, I dare say? You should get off, now, eh?'

Billy's eyes slid back to the angel. The ray of sunlight had moved on and Billy stared up at her carved face. Now he saw that the grime of years had striped her face with dark marks like tears and that her hair was covered in green lichen. How had he not noticed? Confused, Billy turned back to the old man, but he had moved on too, whistling as he bumped his wheelbarrow over the yew roots that criss-crossed the path towards the gate of the graveyard.

At least he won't be staying to find out that I'll be hanging around here for as long as I can, thought Billy.

It was only as Billy listened to the rattle and clatter of the rake in the wheelbarrow that he wondered where the old man had come from and why he hadn't heard him approach at all.

CHAPTER NINE

31st October, St Giles Academy, 11 a.m.

Mrs Walls had finished compiling the lists of absences from the morning registers. Cross-checking the list of emails and phone calls that came in from parents each morning to say that their children wouldn't be present for this or that reason against the twenty-five class registers was one of her main tasks each day. She was methodical. No truant ever escaped her notice. Each parent was to be notified if their child was not at school when they should be and a strict record of attendance over the year was kept in order to identify problem children or families.

She was used to some familiar names cropping up and to typing in the same parents' email addresses before writing 'It has come to our attention that........... has an unauthorized absence.' But today she was surprised to see Billy McKenna on the list. He was such a good boy! So quiet and polite and his mum always contacted school if he was unwell. Sighing, she moved away from her neat piles of registers and the careful lists in her notebook and turned to her screen to look for Billy's mother's email address.

Just then James Johnson and Max Hilliard burst into the office.

'Got a bleeder here, Mrs Walls!' laughed Max, and James snorted too, spreading a combination of snot and his nose bleed across the paperwork on her desk . . .

CHAPTER TEN

The day was passing too slowly. Billy sat with his back to the pillbox, not in the graveyard, but on the other side of the boundary, overlooking a field of scrubland. The autumn sun was warm now. Billy sat on his coat, a piece of the loaf and an empty packet of cheese at his side. His book was open but Billy wasn't taking in any of the words. His gaze kept wandering over the field, watching the occasional dog walker or cyclist pass on the other side.

I can see them but they have no idea that I am here, he thought, *which is just as well.*

Billy watched the crows swirling above the treetops and the clouds drifting overhead. A runner flashed into view and away again. Ducks flew noisily across the skyline.

He was bored.

And restless.

His thoughts kept jumping about. He wondered what would happen later when his mother would be expecting him to get in from school.

Often in the evenings she would have already set off for a night shift at the care home and he would have to let himself in. On a good day Jeff would be working a late shift so Billy would have the house to himself. The bad days were when Jeff came home after a few pints in the pub after work and it was just the two of them in the house. Billy dreaded Jeff coming up to his room, hovering in the doorway, his eyes scanning the room to try to find fault with Billy in some way – a sock here or unfolded uniform there. But Billy knew to keep everything shipshape and make himself small and quiet and to focus on his homework. And to wait for his mum to come home.

The worst days were when his mum *was* home and Jeff was home too. Then Jeff didn't bother coming upstairs to try to find fault with Billy because he was so good at finding it with the tiniest thing Billy's mum did. Like last night.

But what about tonight? Surely the school would have called her to say Billy hadn't been in class? Would his mum know he was gone yet? He hoped not because he didn't want to think about how upset she'd be.

Or what Jeff would say.

Or do.

He knew that by leaving he had probably made a bad situation worse for his mum. The thought of it made him feel sick.

But Billy also knew that he couldn't have carried on with his life as it was. He just couldn't *bear* one more day of seeing or hearing her misery. He didn't want to make things *more* difficult for her, but he wanted to have other thoughts, other images to call to mind. In his head the rows he had heard played over and over again like a film. Snippets of scenes he had overheard or glimpsed slid in and out of his mind. He wanted to block it all out. He wanted it to stop.

If he was bigger, stronger, older maybe, he could have *done* something, *said* something. Stood up to Jeff.

But he wasn't.

He couldn't.

He was helpless.

He was just a small, quiet runaway, sitting in a field by All Souls' graveyard, watching the birds circle overhead.

He felt safe here. At home he was always on edge. Always nervous. Vigilant. Here that had eased away. He watched the birds dip and dive over the trees. He felt guilty for making his mum's situation worse by leaving but he had such a strong feeling of relief to be here. Hiding. Away from it all.

As long as this place stayed a secret he would be safe.

Billy picked up his book and read another chapter. The breeze rustled the ivy leaves. It was calm. Quiet.

But what was that?

A rustling. It was more than the breeze. He was sure of it.

It was a regular swishing through leaves.

And it was *very* close by.

Was it getting closer?

Hurriedly Billy bundled up the bread and book in his coat and slipped under the ivy and into the safety of his hideaway. He stood silently, trying to control his breathing. Tiptoeing up to the small rectangular holes that served as windows, Billy peered through the leaves and into the graveyard beyond.

He couldn't see anything. Just the tops of gravestones above the undergrowth.

But he *could* hear something. That regular swooshing and scraping again.

Billy shifted to the other window and peered out between the ivy leaves.

At first there was nothing. And then he saw the bend of a back. The shape of a man appeared from behind a headstone, rising and straightening as if emerging from out of the ground.

Billy's heart thumped.

It was him! The old man who had given him the hankie that morning. He was stretching out his back, hands on hips, facing away from Billy. It was the same checked shirt and green cords. He had thought that the old man had left hours ago but all this time Billy's hiding place had been so close to being discovered!

Even though he was safely hidden inside the pillbox, Billy held his breath.

Don't make a sound.

The old man reached down and took up the handles of a wheelbarrow from behind the gravestone. He walked a few steps, as if heading away from where Billy was hiding.

And then he stopped.

Slowly he put the wheelbarrow down, then he turned and stared directly at the pillbox.

Oh no, oh no, oh no!

'C'mon then, lad. Come out!' he called.

Billy panicked.

'C'mon. Don't spend your day hiding away. Come out!'

Billy stepped out of the pillbox. It was the only thing to do. He stood awkwardly between the trees. The old man faced him across the mess of nettles and brambles.

'So, you've been here all day, 'ave you? What are you doin' in there? Ain't you a bit old to be playin' camps?'

The old man peered at Billy through narrowed eyes.

'I . . . um . . . I . . .' Billy's heart was thumping. He didn't know what to say.

'Won't someone be expecting you home soon?'

'Yes, but . . . please. *Please* don't tell anyone I'm here. *Please* don't tell anyone that you've seen me. Don't make me go back! I can't!'

The words began to gush from Billy.

'Please. I just need a bit of . . . time.'

'Oh aye? Time is it? You young folk will talk about "needing time" and "having head space".'

The man shook his head slowly without taking his eyes off Billy's face.

'Well, I don't know about needing time but I do know fear when I see it. And I see it in you, lad. You ain't playing camps, are you? You're hiding in there.' The old man nodded towards the pillbox. 'I thought when I saw you this morning that you looked a bit rough. No wonder if you're sleeping in there. Isn't there somewhere warmer you could go? Someone I could phone for you?'

'I . . . I j . . . just need a few days . . .' stammered Billy. '*Please* don't tell anyone I'm here.'

He glanced about him as if others were already closing in on him. The old man watched him steadily.

'Well, I suppose for all you look like a fox startled by hounds, you must be pretty plucky, or pretty desperate to hide in a place like this. I'll do you a deal. It so happens that I have a few busy days of work here. What do you say to helping me out and I keep quiet about you being here? Just for one or two days, mind.'

He turned on his heels and picked up the wheelbarrow again.

'C'mon then!' he called over his shoulder.

Billy watched as the old man settled at a tree and started to cut away at the branches with long-handled seca-teurs. Not knowing what to do, Billy hesitated behind him, glimpsing the almost hidden gravestones that the tree had twisted round. The man tugged and muttered as branch after branch was stripped away. 'Don't just stand there, lad, take these to that pile over there. Make yourself useful!'

So Billy picked up one branch after another and carried or dragged them over to the corner of the graveyard, again and again and again. It seemed to take hours before the gravestone was free from the

53

cluster of branches. The man had cut an archway framing
the stone and was on his knees, tugging at handfuls of ivy
round the base.

Billy moved closer. Over the old man's shoulder he read
on the crumbling headstone:

Here lies
Reverend Thomas Caldwell
1794–1875
At rest

'Why are you doing this? Surely it should be people in
high-vis jackets working through this lot with strimmers?
Shouldn't the council be doing it? Or is that a family grave?'

'This old place is just looked after by volunteers supposedly. But people are so busy these days, ain't they? Not many find the time. No, these aren't *all* my family but they *are* my friends and I like it to look nice for them. I've done it for the captain and his family over there.' He pointed. 'And the Spicer sisters there and the Collins there and young Private Ernest Engles over there . . . There's so much to do and so little time!'

As he gestured around the graveyard Billy noticed, among the tall grass and nettles, that a neat passageway had been carved through the undergrowth round the graveyard and that more of the headstones were tidy and weed-free.

Billy didn't quite get it or see why there was a rush to get it done but he had to keep his side of the deal and he was glad to be busy – it kept his mind off his troubles. He knelt down alongside his gruff companion and started to clear the weeds and ivy from the next grave. And, as the crows cawed and swirled overhead, preparing to roost in the trees above the graveyard for the night, the only other sound to be heard was the swooshing and scraping of undergrowth being cleared away.

CHAPTER ELEVEN

31st October, 24 Brownsfield Close, 6.30 p.m.

The key slid into the lock and Grace stepped wearily into the hall. It had been a long and a tiring shift. Her limbs felt slow and heavy as she unbuttoned her coat and hung it up. She slipped off her trainers and her socks and pulled her work tabard over her head. It had food stains down it from Mavis, who had struggled to swallow her dinner, and dried orange juice from when Mavis's husband, Albert, had thrown his cup at them both in temper.

'Hello?' she called up the stairs.

No reply.

Jeff must be down the pub. She sighed with relief and shrugged some of the tension out of her shoulders.

Grace plodded wearily along the hall. *I need a cuppa*, she thought. But with her hand on the kitchen door handle she stopped. The house was unusually quiet. Something was wrong. It was too quiet. Where was Billy? She turned back and noticed that his coat was not hanging beside hers. His shoes were not in the rack beneath.

'Billy?'

Quickening her pace she went upstairs. Billy was *always* in. He didn't go to after school clubs. He didn't 'hang out' with other kids. He was always here. Quiet, steady, dependable Billy. Her Billy. Her boy.

She opened the door to his room. It was empty, as she already knew it would be.

'Billy?'

She thought over her day in her mind. When had she last seen him? Which day? This morning at breakfast? No. Yesterday? No. Hurrying downstairs she checked the answer machine in the hall for messages. None. She scrabbled in her handbag for her mobile. No missed calls. No messages. She called his number.

And from upstairs she heard the buzz of Billy's mobile echoing through the empty house.

Chapter Twelve

Billy and the old man had worked until it was too dark to do any more. The autumnal winds rustled the branches above their heads and leaves danced and scattered around them. A robin hopped nearby, his beady eye looking out for the worms and beetles that had been tugged up in the tangle of weeds they had cleared. Billy had dirt on his knees and under his nails and blisters on his hands from cutting back the undergrowth. He had been so absorbed in his task that he had barely noticed that the afternoon had slipped into evening.

The old man had walked back and forth with his wheelbarrow, carrying off piles of weeds and brambles and returning to fill the barrow again. He hadn't talked much to

Billy except to point him in the direction of one headstone in need of attention after another, with comments such as 'Young Marion, she always liked things proper. Would have gone on to be a great scientist if it weren't for that old man of hers,' or 'That ivy will need cutting back; you can barely see the names of those young nippers of Sanjeev's,' or 'Lovely Eva. Shame her family moved away'. More often he seemed to mutter to himself: 'I'll never get it done in time,' or 'Every year the same and I'm not getting any younger.' And sometimes to the stones themselves: 'Not long now, Mabel. We'll get everything looking just right for you.'

He was an odd character, thought Billy, but he seemed kind for all his gruffness and Billy was grateful for the company.

The light had turned to the blue-grey of early evening when the man stood up, stretched his back and announced, 'That's enough for one day, I think, lad.'

Together they surveyed their handiwork. A corner of the graveyard was now tidy. The shapes of stones set off against neatly trimmed shrubs or bushes, each stone surrounded by halos of cropped fresh grass.

'More tomorrow?' the man asked as he wiped the dirt from his tools. 'I'll meet you here bright and early. We've still got plenty to do and it's good for you to keep busy, lad. There's a tap over there; why don't you go and clean yourself up a bit?'

Billy scrubbed his hands under the freezing water, scratching the ground-in dirt with his nails. It was only when he turned back to the graveyard that he realized just how much the gloom had set in. He stepped back along the path to where the old man had been. There was no sign of him at all.

No wheelbarrow. No tools.

No one.

He had disappeared.

Billy shrugged and picked his way back towards the pillbox, suddenly feeling very small, tired and alone. As he pushed aside the ivy that covered the entrance he stumbled against something at his feet. Billy reached down and picked up an old drawstring bag. Once inside he lit a candle and settled down to see what was in the bag. His fingers closed round a squat thermos flask. An elastic band held a piece of paper and a spoon to the side. Delving into the bag again he pulled out the torch he had dropped last night and a checked woollen blanket. Billy wrapped it round his shoulders and slipped the paper from the flask.

It was a note . . .

IF YOU'RE KEEPING YOUR SIDE OF THE DEAL, YOU'LL NEED TO KEEP YOUR STRENGTH UP.

Billy unscrewed the lid. It was a flask of stew. A warm dinner.

He stood in the doorway of the pillbox looking out through the ivy and over the field in the blue of the early night sky. The cosy woollen blanket still wrapped round his shoulders. Slowly he spooned the warm stew into his mouth and his whole body was flooded with the glow of knowing that someone was looking out for him.

That old man had been so thoughtful. So kind.

Curious old chap, Billy thought, as he stretched and stepped into his hideaway for the night.

Chapter Thirteen

31st October, 24 Brownsfield Close, 6.45 p.m.

Grace tapped Jeff's number into her mobile.

'The person at this number is currently unavailable. Please leave your message after the tone . . .'

She tried again straight away and got the same voice message.

'Jeff. It's me . . . Call me! I don't know what to do. It's Billy . . . Call me back.'

She clicked off the phone.

Should she wait for Jeff to call?

What if he doesn't?

What if he doesn't hear her message?

She stepped out of the front door and looked around the street. All those houses with lights on. All those people living so close, whose houses she walked past every day, and she didn't know any of them. All those people who could have seen Billy. Who might know where he is. *We don't need them others*, Jeff had always said, holding her a bit too tightly. *We've got each other.* His voice was so clear in her head that she actually hesitated.

Then she thought of Billy.

Well, I need someone now! thought Grace.

Should she call the police? Her mind rushed back to the time, years ago, when she had watched helplessly as two young constables laughed and joked as they climbed back into their police car, Jeff's hand gripping her already bruised arm tightly as he waved them away. His hissed whisper in her ear as the door closed behind them, 'That is the first and last time you'll ever call the police. Do you understand?'

She had understood.

But now. What should she do?

Grace clenched her jaw, took a deep breath and stepped over the shrubs that separated their house from the neighbour's and knocked on the door.

The light went on in the hallway and Grace saw the silhouette of a figure walking towards her.

Please hurry, she thought.

A key clicked in the lock and a young woman peeped out from a crack in the opened door.

'Oh, hello!' she said, opening the door wider to reveal her neat hair, a grey skirt and pink nails. 'It's you from next door, isn't it?' She smiled. 'I'm so glad to meet you. I've been meaning to pop over and say "hi". Um . . . are you all right? Is everything okay?' The woman peered past Grace as if to check to see whether anyone else was there. 'Are you on your own? Do you want to come in?'

The door opened wider and Grace felt a rush of relief.

'Y . . . yes! Yes I do,' stuttered Grace as she stepped on to the doormat. 'Thank you.'

She looked at the young woman, searching for the right words . . .

'I need your help.

Please.

It's my Billy.

He's gone.'

CHAPTER FOURTEEN

Billy had made himself cosy. He had lit some candles and lined them up on the stone ledges inside each tiny window. He had wrapped himself in the blanket, snuggled down inside his sleeping bag and finished the stew. It had been comforting. Warming him from the inside. The combination of being out in the fresh air all afternoon and the sensation of being well fed made him feel drowsy. And now he felt safe and warm in the flickering candlelight, cocooned from the dark night.

Instead of the sound of Jeff's heavy footsteps on the stairs, there was the occasional hoot of an owl. Instead of the rumble of Jeff's voice, there was the rush of the night breeze in the trees outside. He felt a greater sense of comfort out

here in a pillbox in a graveyard, in the dark, than he did in his own home.

Until he heard the snap of a twig outside . . .

Then the rustling of footsteps in the tangle of ivy and brambles.

Billy held his breath.

Someone was there.
Right outside the pillbox.

He scrambled to peep out of the slots in the stone, but the candlelight was too strong to see anything out there.

He blew hurriedly at the flames and in the sudden darkness he looked out again . . .

He was looking straight into a face that was peering in through the ivy.

Chapter Fifteen

31st October, 26 Brownsfield Close, 6.47 p.m.

'Okay. So let me just check this . . .'

The young woman was calm and laid a steady hand on Grace's arm.

'Billy is your son? . . . And Billy . . . isn't home? He's taken his pillow but not his mobile. You last saw him the day before yesterday teatime but he could have slipped out at any point after that. You don't know when he left?'

'Yes. That's it.' Grace's eyes darted nervously. 'I don't know what to do. It's so unlike him.'

'That's okay. I think the first thing we should do is call the police . . .'

'No! Please, no!' Grace looked desperate. '*We* don't call the police. Jeff wouldn't want me to.'

The memory of the sounds she had heard through the wall last night flooded back to the young woman and the vision of the man smoking at the end of the garden path. And was that the hint of a bruise on her neighbour's cheek under the make-up? *If it is then I can see why he wouldn't want the police called*, she thought . . .

'Okay . . .' she said slowly. 'We don't need to do that yet if you don't want to. 'Maybe we can check with the other neighbours in the street first? Let's see if anyone else saw Billy yesterday, or this morning, just in case. And if not, then we'll have to call the police, okay?'

She looked down at Grace's bare feet.

'You go back and put some shoes on and get a jacket. I'll change out of my work clothes and we'll go round together. I'll leave the front door on the latch so you can come in when you've got your stuff.'

Grace twitched a brief smile of relief.

The young woman held Grace's gaze and smiled back.

'Go on, get your stuff and bring your phone – you'll have a photo of Billy on it, won't you?'

Grace nodded as she headed out of the door.

'Oh, I'm Suzie, by the way . . .'

CHAPTER SIXTEEN

'Hello?' called a voice.

Billy stepped back to the middle of his hideaway.

It definitely wasn't the old man. It was a young voice.

He'd been discovered. Already! What was he going to *do*? It was too soon.

'Hello?'

The voice was moving round the outside of the pillbox. Billy could hear footsteps rustling through the undergrowth. He felt like a trapped animal, his heart banging furiously in his chest.

Now the voice was at the other window.

'Hello?

Hello?

I can see you, you know!'

Billy circled helplessly, hopelessly, not knowing what to do.

'Look, I know you're in there. Why don't you just come out? Or maybe I can come in? Where's the entrance?'

Oh no! Not in here. This was *his* place. *His* hideaway. Billy shrugged off the blanket, clicked on his torch and stepped out through the ivy-covered doorway.

'Billy! Billy McKenna! I knew it was you!'

It was a slight girl with tight black curls, eyes wide and mouth open in surprise.

Billy knew her. She was from school.

'I can't believe it's you!' She almost whispered, amazement in her voice.

Then the memories of the girl's blushing face as she was moved to sit next to him in maths came tumbling back. He had kept his head down as always and barely looked at her, but he still remembered jeers and whistles from James Johnson and Max Hilliard at the back of the room.

'Oh, um, hi, Izzie,' he mumbled.

'What are you doing in there?'

Billy stood awkwardly. 'Um . . . I . . . I was just . . . um . . .' The words were stuck.

'Have you made, like, a *den*?' The girl stepped round him. 'What even *is* this place? How on earth did you find it? How d'you get in? I've been round this place loads of times and I totally never realized there was anything here except a load of ivy!'

She was sweeping away at the leaves that covered the outside of the pillbox.

'Wow! There's a doorway. This is *so* cool!'

Before Billy knew what was happening she had stepped through the ivy and into the pillbox.

His pillbox.

'No! Wait! Don't . . .' Billy stumbled after her. 'Please, I . . .'

It was dark inside, so Billy reached for the matches on one of the windowsills and lit a few of the candles again.

'No waaayy! This is *totally mad*!' the girl whispered as the flickering flames lit the room. 'This is *super* cool! How did you find this place?' Her voice wavered as she took in the neatly made bed, the orderly pile of books and the rucksack hanging from the string suspended across the room. There was an awkward silence as she took it all in.

'Wait. You're not . . . um . . . *living* here are you? *Seriously?* Why?'

'Well, not exactly . . .' Billy mumbled.

'But you're *sleeping* here? And *eating* here? That looks like living here to me.' Her eyes were round as she took in the candles and the folded clothes. 'And you weren't in maths today either. Wait. What's going on? Are you okay?' The smile had fallen away from her face and she suddenly looked serious. 'Billy, no one knows you're here, do they?'

Chapter Seventeen

31st October, Brownsfield Close, 7.15 p.m.

Grace and Suzie stood together waiting for the door to be opened.

'Who is it? What do you want?' called a voice from inside. 'I don't do that *trick-or-treat* nonsense, so if you've come for sweets you can go hop it!'

'No. We haven't come because it's Halloween. We're your neighbours. Could we speak to you a moment? I'm Suzie from number twenty-six and I'm with Grace from number twenty-four.'

Both women exchanged a glance of relief as they heard the catch slide back on the door. An old stern-looking woman with a pouting bottom lip opened the door a fraction.

Grace held out a photo of Billy on her phone.

'It's my son. My Billy. He's gone missing. Maybe run away. I wondered if you'd seen him go in or out of number twenty-four yesterday? Or this morning?'

The woman peered at the phone, then up at Grace, and then down the street to number 24. She shifted her watery eyes back to Grace.

'No. I ain't seen your son. And I ain't seen you before either. Number twenty-six you say? Are you new?'

Suzie stepped forward. 'It's number twenty-four. Could you just check your shed or your garage? Maybe he hasn't gone far? That'd be so—'

The door shut in their faces.

'—helpful.'

Grace felt tears in her eyes. She checked her phone for new messages.

'Maybe we should just wait for Jeff to come home? He'll know what to do.'

'Not everyone will be like that, Grace. Come on. Don't lose heart. Let's just check the next few houses. You never know . . .'

All the lights were blazing at number 55 and a lit pumpkin sat on the doorstep. A jolly woman in a cardie and carrying a tub of sweets answered the door.

She smiled.

'Well, you two don't look like trick-or-treaters!'

Grace stepped forward.

'It's my Billy. He's my son. He's only thirteen. He's gone missing. From number twenty-four. I wondered if you'd seen him yesterday or today? He'd have to walk past your house to leave the street . . .'

'Oh. I'm sorry, pet. Really I am. What a worry for you.' The woman peered closely at the phone. 'Lovely-looking boy, isn't he? I wouldn't say I'd noticed him before, though, and definitely not in the last couple of days. Are you sure he's not popped out with his mates for a bit of trick-or-treating?'

The woman looked up into Grace's face. 'Ah, no. I can see you're proper worried.' She reached out and gave Grace's arm a squeeze. 'Give me a mo and I'll get a pen and paper and you can give me your number. I'll call you if I remember anything or see anything.'

Grace wrote her name and mobile number on the scrap of paper and they turned to walk back down the path.

'I know we haven't met before but I'm always here if you need something,' the woman called. 'I'm Lorraine. You can pop round any time.'

'That was better,' smiled Suzie. 'Let's keep going.'

They knocked on one door after another. People were kind and concerned. They checked with their families, took Grace's number and offered to look in their gardens, garages and sheds, while Grace anxiously checked her phone. There was no reply from Jeff. And no one remembered seeing Billy. Ever. They didn't even recognize him from the photo.

The two women stood looking up and down the cul-de-sac.

'That's it then,' said Suzie. 'No one has seen him.'

She looked sideways at Grace.

'Not many of them recognize you either. I thought we hadn't met because I'm new here but you really do keep yourself to yourself, don't you?'

She watched as Grace checked her phone *again*.

'I think it is time we called the police, Grace, don't you?'

CHAPTER EIGHTEEN

'You have, haven't you? OMG! You've run away from home! What did you *do*? Are you in some sort of massive trouble? Have your parents kicked you out?'

Izzie barely gave Billy a chance to answer. He pushed past her into the cold night air looking nervously around.

'Are you here on your own, Izzie? I kind of didn't want to be seen . . .'

But as he spoke he realized that the lights of the chapel were on and that the trees were lit with warm light from the glowing windows.

'What's going on in there?' asked Billy.

There were one or two cars parked near the front of the chapel and a bike propped up against the wall. How had he not heard them arrive?

'It's choir night. My mum comes to sing. She says it helps her let off steam. Her job is *soooo* stressful. I'm supposed to be sitting at the back of the chapel drawing for my art homework but I got bored and decided to go for a wander. I'm not bored now! I've just found Billy McKenna hiding in a spooky graveyard!'

'How did you see I was here?'

'Dur! You've lit candles in the windows. You've given yourself away! Bit of a schoolboy error!'

Billy looked back at the mound of ivy and could see the flickering yellow light deep beneath the leaves. He darted back in and blew them out before joining her outside at the edge of the graveyard.

Billy nodded towards the chapel. 'I thought it was unused, you know, decommissioned or whatever they call it?'

'It is,' said Izzie. 'And it's empty *most* of the time. I think a few clubs use it sometimes, like the choir. It isn't a church choir. They're not religious. They sing loads of different stuff.'

As if on cue the sound of singing began to swell from the chapel.

'Don't worry – they're so busy in there, they won't think to come looking for you out here!'

Billy and Izzie leant against a couple of gravestones as the sound of a sweet and sad song pulsed through the air. Billy was mesmerized. His heart slowed as he listened, his eyes fixed on the shapes of yellow light in the silhouette of the small dark building. One round of voices overlapped another as a throb of sorrow filled the graveyard.

They both stood in silence and listened.

When it had ebbed away and the sound of the night returned to the graveyard, Izzie turned to Billy.

'Er, are you okay?' she asked.

And for the second time that day Billy realized that he was crying. At least his eyes were full of tears and one spilled over and ran down his cheek. He couldn't look at Izzie.

Embarrassed, she rummaged in her pocket and rustled some crumpled paper. 'Here. Have some chocolate . . .'

There was an awkward silence as they chomped on squares of chocolate and Billy wiped his eyes on his sleeve.

'Look. I am in trouble . . . but . . . um . . . I haven't done anything wrong. It's just that . . . um . . . being at home is . . .' He couldn't find the words. 'It's . . . difficult.'

'My mum can be a pain but it wouldn't make me want to hang out here overnight!' said Izzie.

'Exactly! That's my point,' said Billy. 'It's bad. I really, really can't go home. Not yet. I really need him not to know I am here, okay?'

She stared at him steadily. Unsure. 'Him?'

'Please. *Please don't tell anyone you've seen me,*' Billy begged.

'Just for now. I need some time.'

The faint ring of a mobile sounded from inside the chapel, followed by a groan.

'Izzie? *Izzie!* Are you out here?'

Billy and Izzie stepped swiftly back into the shadow of the trees.

'It's my mum!' she whispered.

'IZZIE! Don't mess me about! We've got to go! I've had a call from work. Where *are* you? Izzie!'

'*Please!*' hissed Billy as Izzie made to go. '*Please* don't say ANYTHING about me being here. I just need some time! Just a few days . . .

PLEASE! Promise me.'

But she was already halfway across the graveyard.

Chapter Nineteen

31st October, 24 Brownsfield Close, 9.30 p.m.

'So, Ms McKenna, while my colleague is doing a quick search here to check Billy isn't hiding somewhere in this property,' said the young PC, 'can I just run through this again to check that I have all the correct information?'

She glanced up from her notebook at the woman on the sofa opposite. She was sitting with her hands clenched in her lap, her eyes unblinking, completely still except for the twitching nerve beneath her left eye. She looked incredibly tired. And incredibly scared. But then you would be, wouldn't you, if your son had gone missing? Another woman with pink nail varnish stepped out of the kitchen and passed them both mugs of tea, then perched on the arm of the sofa.

'You last saw Billy on . . .' She flicked back through the

pages of her notebook, 'the twenty-ninth of October? That was two days ago. Can you tell me why you hadn't called us before?'

'Well. I didn't realize he wasn't here. I do shifts. Sometimes we don't see each other for a day or so . . .'

'Okay. So on the twenty-ninth you and he had tea together after he got back from school? Can you tell me what you talked about?'

'I don't know. Nothing really. I told him about my shift at work. He told me about his day at school. He was just normal.'

'Did Billy tell you anything unusual about his day at school? Did he get into trouble? Did he fall out with his friends?'

'No. Nothing like that. Billy's never in trouble. He's a good boy.'

'What about his friends? Who do you think we could talk to about Billy at school?'

'Well, no one really. He doesn't mention any friends.'

'Does anyone come round to call for him? Does he go out? Who would he be out trick-or-treating with tonight, for instance?'

'No. No one. He wouldn't be out at all. He's just here. All the time. With me. That's how I know something's wrong.'

'Okay. So you saw Billy at teatime and then you went to work and Billy had gone to school when you got up and you didn't see him that night? The thirtieth? Why is that? Were you working late?'

'Er . . . no. I was here. Billy was in his room. I'm sure he was.'

'But you didn't see him? Why is that?'

'Well . . .'

The young constable knew from her training to leave a silence if you want an answer. So she waited, half listening to the groups of children outside passing from one house to another.

'It's just that . . .'

'Yes?'

'That . . .' Grace fell silent.

'Grace,' said Suzie gently. 'I think I know what happened that night. I could hear from next door . . .'

'What did happen, Grace?' asked the constable.

Both women looked expectantly at Grace.

'I . . .'

Then there was the sound of a click in the lock in the hall. Grace jumped. The front door opened and a wiry, compact man with a receding hairline stepped through the doorway of the sitting room. He made a swift scan of the group of women, extended his hand and, with a wide smile on his face, said, 'I'm Jeff Lansdale. What's happening here and what can I do to help?'

Chapter Twenty

Billy stumbled behind Izzie as she ran through the graveyard towards the waiting car, its interior light illuminating
the woman in the driving seat as she tapped something
into her mobile. He hesitated at the edge of the row of yew
trees, keen not to be seen and frustrated at not knowing for
sure if his secret was safe. He watched as Izzie opened the

car, slipped into the passenger seat and closed the
door with a clunk. Izzie put her earbuds in, lowered
her window and gazed out into the night.

Surely she wouldn't be able to see him here amongst the
branches of yew?

If Izzie could see him, so could her mum,
but luckily she seemed too busy with her
phone. The sound of a ringtone buzzed out
from the car, breaking the eerie silence. The
woman indicated to Izzie to close the
window and answered the call with a
weary, 'Sergeant Chorley here.'

'It's a schoolkid who lives in Brownsfield Close. He's thirteen. Hasn't been seen for sure for two days. Good kid, apparently. Never given anyone any cause for concern before. I've circulated his description to the night shift and we've posted that he's missing on Facebook. I'd normally just wait for the briefing tomorrow morning but I wanted to speak to you before I clock off for the night. I'd like to talk it through. There's something not quite right at home . . .'

Sergeant Chorley felt her palms tingle with foreboding.

'What makes you say that?'

'Well, at first I was there asking the mum about her missing son and he didn't sound like he was a real teenager. No friends. No clubs. No trouble.'

'Okay . . . ?'

There was a question in Sergeant Chorley's voice. She absent-mindedly scanned groups of trick-or-treaters as they passed by the end of the lane to the graveyard, jostling along the pavement, buckets in hand, ghoulish make-up shining out under the street lights.

'What else?'

'I didn't think much of it to start off with. I think that the mum and her friend were about to tell me something but

92

then her bloke came home. His name is –' a pause here while the PC flicked through her notes, '– Jeff Lansdale.'

'What about him?'

'Well, seemed like a nice bloke. Helpful. Friendly.'

'Hardly incriminating, though. So . . . ?'

'He didn't know anything about the boy being missing so they hadn't had chance to talk about it. He was really concerned and was all help and smiles.'

'Do you think this bloke, Jeff, has something to do with the boy's disappearance?'

'I'm not sure. But there's something not right there, sarge. It wasn't what he said or did, it was her, the mum, Grace. As soon as Jeff walked in her body language changed. Before he arrived she was worried, obviously, but helpful, keen to talk. But as soon as the boyfriend walked in she didn't say a word. She barely made eye contact. He answered everything. Once he was home there was no way I could get her on her own to ask more questions. To get a better idea of what's going on. It's all on my body cam so you'll be able to see what I mean.'

'Okay. Thanks. Can you hang on there before going off shift? I'm coming back in and will be there in ten minutes.'

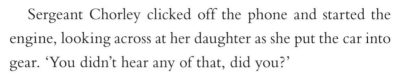

Sergeant Chorley clicked off the phone and started the engine, looking across at her daughter as she put the car into gear. 'You didn't hear any of that, did you?'

'Sorry, what?' asked Izzie as she pulled her earbuds out. 'Did you say something?'

'No. Just that I have to go back in to work. Something's come up.'

'No worries,' Izzie sighed, 'Shall I sort out some dinner for when you get home?'

'That'd be great, darling. I'll drop you off and just go in for an hour or so.'

Billy stood in the shadows and watched the car pull gently away and bump down the lane. He felt certain that Izzie was seeking him out against the trees as he saw her face pass by, pressed against the passenger window.

Then she was gone.

Chapter Twenty-One

31st October, 24 Brownsfield Close, 10.45 p.m.

Grace sat and stared out at the street. The trick-or-treaters had long since gone, and most of the windows were dark. Occasionally a cat triggered a porch light as it slunk between houses, but otherwise all was quiet.

Where are you, Billy?

Come home. Come back to me.

But as she sat there she knew that even if she didn't know *where* Billy had gone, she knew *why*. Somehow she had hoped that she had managed to protect Billy from the worst of what her life had become, but, of course, he was here in the house with them both day after day. She thought back to the happy and carefree boy he had been before they had moved in with Jeff. How long had it been since she had seen an unguarded expression on his face? More than months. Years.

He deserves better, she thought.

Jeff had let Suzie and the police constable out with the usual charm and handshakes, saying that he was sure Billy would be home soon. But the second the door clicked shut behind them he had turned to Grace, hissing that she was making a fool of herself and that Billy was just attention-seeking and asking what kind of mother would let her son just slip away like that? He told her that it was no wonder that Billy had left – he was probably ashamed of having such a pathetic excuse of a human being for a mother, that he was probably embarrassed by her.

'Have you actually been out, going from house to house, looking like that?' Jeff's eyes swept with disdain over Grace's clothes, and he tutted, shaking his head.

'I can't believe I took you and that brat of yours in. Biggest mistake of my life.' Then he turned and stomped into the kitchen, making a bacon butty and complaining about the lack of a 'proper' tea. When he had eaten he sloped off to watch telly in bed.

I deserve better, thought Grace.

Wherever you are, Billy, I hope you are safe and are sleeping well . . .

Chapter Twenty-Two

Billy awoke with a start.

He lay there in the dark, his ears straining to pick up the sound of whatever had woken him. There it was. The shriek of a girl outside. Jumping up, Billy reached for the torch and without turning it on, he tried to see what was happening in the graveyard. It wasn't just one girl. It was five or six older kids dressed up in Halloween costumes, some of them carrying torches. One boy was lighting up the inside of a carved pumpkin head and was chasing the others between the gravestones with it. The others laughed and yelped and lunged about, pretending to be disgusted and frightened of the head. Billy watched as they dropped the pumpkin to the

ground and kicked it about between them, bits of it scattering as it disintegrated beneath their feet. When there was nothing left they leant against gravestones and laughed as they shone torches under their faces, jesting in over-loud voices that echoed around the quiet of the graveyard. Before long they made their way over to the trees by the pillbox.

Please don't let them be heading here! thought Billy, holding his breath. *Don't let them find me!*

He couldn't bear the thought of even more people knowing he was there. Two was already too many in his opinion, but there was nothing he could do about that now. He couldn't bear the thought of having to go home. It was too soon. And he was afraid of the ridicule if they found him. The trouble they would surely make. *They* wouldn't keep his secret. He was sure of it.

But they all crashed past his hideaway, heading through the gaps in the trees to the field beyond. Except one.

The last boy drew level with the pillbox and hesitated, looking back over his shoulder to the graveyard.

Billy could hardly breathe.

'Hey, Em. Wait up!' the boy called.

Billy exhaled. He was okay. It wasn't about him.

One girl peeled off from the group and headed back to where the boy was waiting.

'What? What is it? The others are going, you know.'

The two were standing so near to the pillbox that Billy could almost reach out and touch them. He could *see* their breath.

'I just thought that we don't need to hang out with all of them, you know.'

'Nah, Josh. I'm good, thanks. Let's catch up with the others. I'm cold.'

'I'll warm you up. Come here! I like it more when it's just us. You know what I mean?'

'No, Josh. I don't. I mean, we're friends, yeah? But . . .'

'But, Em, I really like you. You *know* I do.'

'I like you too, just not . . . um . . . like that,' the girl replied.

'You don't get it, Em. I *really, really* like you.'

Billy watched as the boy reached out and took the girl's arm.

She took a step back.

'No, Josh! I'm not interested. We're just friends. Come on, let's go.'

'Why don't you listen to me, Em? I really like you! We'd be good together! Come on!'

'Come on, what, Josh? I said "No!" Let go of my arm! You're hurting me! Just get off, Josh!'

Oh no! He's one of them. Like Jeff. A bully who can't take the word 'no'.

Billy shifted to look out from the other window. The group of friends were distant at the edge of the field. He needed to do something.

'I just want to show you how crazy I am about you. I really want you, Em. You make me want to—'

'No, Josh! Get off!'

Billy watched the boy lunge at the girl, pressing her against a tree trunk, his face against hers, his hands roaming.

Before he had time to think, Billy darted through the ivy and out into the night air. In two strides he was behind them. He shone the torch beam directly into Josh's face and roared, 'Didn't you hear what she said? She said NO!'

The girl screamed, struggled free, gave Josh a hearty shove and staggered back into the field, shouting for her friends and stumbling away through the undergrowth as fast as she could. Josh had tripped and lay looking up, dazzled by the torch beam. Mouth agape. Terrified.

'She didn't *make* you do anything!' Billy shouted, towering over the boy, his rage pulsing through him as he watched Josh trying to scrabble away from him. 'You *chose* to do this! You're scum!'

Billy was screaming. His voice cracking.

'She said *NO!*'

Billy could hear shouts coming from across the field as the group of friends ran towards them. Josh struggled to his feet and staggered off to meet them.

Billy clicked off his torch and stepped back behind the trees, watching the drama unfold as Josh reached the group. Their torches weakly scanned the treeline but Billy could tell they were too scared to step nearer or to seek him out.

Billy watched, his chest heaving, his heart thumping, as the group turned and ran.

And he was alone again.

Shaking and full of rage.

Chapter Twenty-Three

1st November, 24 Brownsfield Close, 8.45 a.m.

Sergeant Chorley drained her mug of tea and placed it carefully on the coaster by the armchair. Once again her eyes swiftly scanned the sitting room. The dark wood sideboard with a set of encyclopaedias and an empty glass vase. Grace and Jeff stared out from a photograph in a silver frame. The TV remote controls were lined up neatly within reach of the armchair. Everything was spotless. Not a speck of dust or a fingerprint smear anywhere. Nor any sign that Billy lived there at all, she noted. Her eyes rested back on the couple on the sofa. Grace sat, knees together, on the edge of her seat – twisting a tissue round and round in her hands. Next to her Jeff leant forward, his face full of concern as he answered Chorley's questions.

'So, as Billy hasn't been seen since school on the thirtieth and this seems to be completely out of character, we're taking his disappearance very seriously and we're doing everything we can to find him quickly.'

'You're right. It is out of character,' agreed Jeff. 'He's such a good kid. Never given us any trouble, has he, love? That's why we're both so, so worried and appreciate anything you can do to get him back home to us.'

'Maybe I can pop these mugs back in the kitchen and then have a look at Billy's room. Is that okay?' Chorley looked at Grace as she asked the question, but Jeff replied.

'Of course. His room's upstairs. Second on the left.'

'Perhaps, Mr Lansdale, you could find me a recent photo of Billy that we could use to circulate to the team and the press? It'll be good to have more than one on our files.'

Turning back from leaving the mugs in the sink of the immaculate kitchen (no evidence of Billy in there either: no school timetable on the fridge, no trainers by the back door. Does he even exist, this boy?).

She braced herself for the mess of a teenager's bedroom.

But Billy's room was like nothing she had ever seen before.

No teenager she knew was this tidy. Not only were there no stray socks or scattered schoolbooks but the duvet was stretched out on the bed without a crease. The pillow was gone but a pair of neatly folded pyjamas sat where it would have been. The desk by the window was clear except for an orderly pile of school exercise books and a calculator. She opened a few drawers to see carefully folded clothes and lined up shoes and trainers in the bottom of a cupboard. On the windowsill was a photo of his mother, taken some years ago, her hair catching the light as it was caught by the breeze at some seaside town, eyes twinkling as she smiled into the camera. The bookcase was neatly organized with all the books arranged by series or size, carefully set out to sit in orderly lines on the shelves. They were all a neat 8cm from the shelf edge, except one series . . .

Chorley reached for the Harry Potters that were sticking out from the rest of the row. Sliding them forward she saw a set of thin A6 notebooks hidden at the back of the shelf. She reached for a couple and saw that they were labelled with the date and year in small, neat, careful handwriting on each cover. She flicked to a random page and read the tiny writing. She couldn't believe what she was seeing. She turned to another page and then another and another, skimming the content. She reached for two more of the books. More of the same. What should she do? She should ask permission to take them. Get them properly signed out and bagged as evidence. But she couldn't risk exposing what she had found. Hearing footsteps on the stairs she knew she had to make a decision quickly. Follow procedure? Or put them back?

The footsteps were closer.

She hurriedly grabbed the diaries and stuffed them into her jacket pocket, sliding the Harry Potters back into place.

'Got what you need, Sergeant? Have you found anything useful?'

Jeff stood in the doorway smiling. But the smile didn't reach his eyes.

Chorley smiled steadily. 'No. Not as helpful as I'd hoped it would be,' she lied.

'Only I've got you his last school photo here,' he said.

'Ah, great!' Chorley forced a bright smile. 'I'll take that back to the station with me now.'

She edged past Jeff on to the landing and thanked him for his help.

As Grace showed her out Chorley hesitated.

'I think you're right that he's run away and that does sound so out of character for Billy. We've raised a missing person report, so we'll be dealing with Billy as a high-priority case. It might help if you could send him a message yourself. Do you think you could make a public appeal? It'll spread awareness among the local community and hopefully mean we can get him home to you very soon.'

Grace nodded.

'Of course. I'll do anything. Anything at all.'

Just then the doorbell rang. Grace opened the door.

'Hello, love. It's me, Lorraine, from number fifty-five? We met yesterday when you were asking about your boy. I thought I'd just pop by and see how you're doing?' The woman looked at the three faces standing awkwardly in the hall. 'Ah! You must be Dad. Hello!' Lorraine reached in and gave Jeff's hand a vigorous shake. 'Any news?'

'N . . . N . . . No. N . . . N . . . Not yet,' Grace stammered, 'but this is Sergeant Chorley and the police are looking for Billy . . .' Her voice trailed away.

'Ah! Good! I was going to talk to one of your lot out in the street. Me and the other neighbours have got together a little search party –' she glanced at Grace – 'to help look for that handsome boy of yours—'

'That's so kind,' Jeff interrupted, his smile a little tight, 'but I'm sure he'll be home soon. There's no need to go to all this trouble. I'm sure the sergeant here will find him in no time.'

'We'll be doing all we can,' said Chorley, her voice steady and her smile firm, 'but I think a search party is an excellent idea. Our resources are tight and we'd appreciate any local help, Lorraine.'

Lorraine turned to Jeff. 'I'm sure you'll help us look, won't you, Dad?'

There was the slightest hesitation before Jeff replied. 'Of course. I'll do anything to get our boy home.'

'Well, that's good. He'll soon be back, I'm sure. In the meantime I made you this for your tea tonight.' Lorraine handed over a glass dish with a tea towel over the top.

'It's a lamb casserole. I thought your mind would be on other things . . .'

'That's very kind, thank you,' said Grace as Jeff reached forward and took the dish.

Lorraine looked from Jeff to Chorley and then to Grace again. 'Okay, love. I'll be in touch.' And she turned back down the garden path.

'I'll be off too,' said Chorley. 'I'll call you later about the appeal.'

She could feel Jeff staring at her as she walked down the path and got back into her car.

Chorley waited until the couple had closed the front door and took the set of little notebooks out of her pocket and put them on the passenger seat.

'Oh, Billy,' she said out loud, 'whatever have you been through?'

CHAPTER TWENTY-FOUR

Billy felt as though he had hardly slept at all. Once he had stopped shaking after the Josh and Em thing, a wave of tiredness swept over him, but even after tucking himself down deeply into his sleeping bag, he couldn't drift off. He kept listening out for sounds outside the pillbox. Straining to hear anything beyond the rustling of the trees. What he had seen and heard rushed through his mind – the girl awkwardly trying to get out of the situation, embarrassed, pulling her arm away. 'You make me . . .' Josh had said, but she hadn't at all, had she? *Surely a 'no' is a 'no'?* thought Billy. How much clearer did she need to be? He played it

over and over in his mind. It had all happened so quickly. Then the boy cowering at his feet, afraid. Is that what it felt like to be Jeff? To see someone frightened of you. Billy had felt angry and . . . *powerful*, and that had left him feeling confused. Where had that anger, that strength come from? Was he a bully too?

And then there was the other doubt in his mind. Could any of the group have actually *seen* him? Would they know he was just a kid himself and that he was hiding here in the graveyard?

Billy was peeing into a pile of leaves in the corner of the graveyard when the old man arrived. As before Billy hadn't heard a footstep and jumped out of his skin when a voice behind him said, 'Yep, cold enough out here today,' nodding towards the steam rising from the leaves. 'I've brought you some breakfast, lad, when you're ready.'

Embarrassed, Billy shuffled over to the bench where the man was unpacking the contents of a bag. Unwrapping a package he passed Billy a warm bacon sandwich.

115

'You look rough this morning, lad. Too cold to sleep, were you? Or were you disturbed by the trouble?'

'How did you know there was trouble?'

'I'm guessing *you* didn't scatter these bits of pumpkin all over the place yourself?'

Billy explained about the group of friends. About their messing around and about Josh trying to force himself on Em.

'Ah. A bad 'un. You did the right thing, lad. It's a sad thing that there's them that'll crash through the world thinking they can just take what they want whenever they want it. And *you* stopped him. You should be proud. A boy like that needs to learn that you can't force respect or affection from someone. If he carries on like that, he'll never know how good it feels to have someone you care about gaze up at you with the love that comes from care and attention. Quiet love, my Edith used to call it.'

'Is Edith your wife?'

'Was. She passed on a few years back. You should've seen her. Radiant, she was. Even when her hair was streaked through with grey my heart'd jump to see those blue eyes smile up at me. Tho' it was harder to get a smile from her after we lost our boy.'

'Lost him? What do you mean?' Billy asked.

The old man looked across at Billy.

'He did what you've done, lad.

He ran away.'

Chapter Twenty-Five

1st November, 24 Brownsfield Close, 10.30 a.m.

Jeff shrugged into his high-vis jacket.

'That bloody boy of yours is just attention-seeking, that's all. All this fuss with police and now neighbours crawling around at all hours.'

'They're only trying to help,' protested Grace.

'What? What did you say? I tell you we don't need help!' Jeff's voice was rising. 'It's a family matter and we don't need busybodies poking their noses into our business. And *you* don't need to go round door to door trying to get sympathy either.'

'I'm *not* looking for sympathy. I'm looking for Billy!'

On the other side of the wall Suzie paused as she packed her papers into her bag for the first meeting of the day.

She could hear Jeff's voice getting louder and louder. She thought back to how many times she had heard this through the wall in the short time she had lived in Brownsfield Close and she remembered the concealed bruise on Grace's cheek. She could guess how it would end this time. She had heard *that* through the wall too. But Grace had never said anything to her and Suzie had never actually *seen* anything. How could she be sure what was happening? Jeff had seemed so nice when she had met him – not at all what she had expected.

Then she thought about Grace, trembling on her doorstep with bare feet, and about Billy being out there somewhere. Alone. Frightened.

Suzie picked up her phone and tapped a message to say she would be working from home that day. Then she slid her laptop out of her bag and typed 'domestic abuse' into the search bar. She began to read.

CHAPTER TWENTY-SIX

'What? And he never came home again?' Billy asked. 'He left and you NEVER saw him again?'

The old man shook his head.

'But why?' asked Billy suspiciously, thinking of Jeff. '*Why* would he want to leave you?'

'Ah. It's sad, it is,' the old man shook his head. 'My Edith so wanted a nipper. We tried for years but with no luck. Edith was already greying when she eventually got pregnant. It was a shock, I can tell you! Well, we were old and old-fashioned and my Edith, she'd been brought up strict and in the church and was set in her ways. She never meant anything by it but times had moved on from when we was young. I think she would have kept him by her all his life if she could – *over-protective* I suppose you'd call it now. Once he was old enough he was off, he didn't want to be tied to her apron strings. He wanted to work and travel he said, not to stay on at school, studying. And then one day we got up and he was gone. He'd just packed his bags, written us a hasty note to say he loved us, and gone. And that was that. We'd lost him.'

'And you never saw him again?' asked Billy.

'Nope. We 'ad some letters – sent with no return address, of course. One or two phone calls telling us what he'd been up to and not to worry about him, but you do, don't you? And then nothing.' The old man shook his head slowly, as if he still couldn't believe it. 'There was days I hoped he'd fallen in love and gone to make his own family somewhere and days when I could've brained him for breaking our hearts. We cried for that boy. Why didn't he at least stay in touch with us? We weren't that bad, were we? My Edith never got over the loss. We never knew where he was, so when Edith got ill I couldn't let him know. She died without ever seein' him again.

'I've raged at him in my head. And I long to see him with all my bones. I still seek him out in a busy street and in

crowds on the telly. Everywhere I go. It's an ache that's never gone away.'

The old man was staring out across the graveyard. 'I can't tell you what it feels like not to know if your child is dead or alive. Not to know if you'll ever see them again.'

There was a long pause. And then the sound of a deep sigh as he turned back to Billy.

'So don't you stay here too long, lad. Remember, our deal is only till tomorrow. I don't know what's happened to you and I am sure you've got your reasons – I can see all isn't right with you. But unless she's done something wrong, don't you go and make that Ma of yours suffer like my Edith suffered. Anyway, lad, eat up. We've got work to do. We need all this ready for tomorrow night.'

'What's happening tomorrow night? Is there some kind of event here?'

'You could say that. Tell you what, lad, if you clear those brambles from along that back wall this morning you'll find the grave of the poet. Then it'll be clear what all this is for. Come on, enough chitterty-chat. Let's get to.'

Then the man passed Billy some gloves and some clippers and disappeared among the stones.

Chapter Twenty-Seven

1st November, 24 Brownsfield Close, 2 p.m.

Grace saw Chorley's car pull up in the street. She put on her mac and stepped outside.

Suzie darted out from number 26.

'Grace, wait! Take this. Read it when you're on your own.' The two women glanced at each other fleetingly as Suzie pressed an envelope into Grace's hand before heading back into her house.

'Jeff went to work,' explained Grace as she climbed into the passenger seat of Sergeant Chorley's car, shaking the rain from her coat before shutting the door. 'I texted him and he'll meet us there.'

Really? thought Chorley. *His partner's son is missing and he went to work?*

But what she said out loud was, 'Great.'

Actually she was relieved. 'We get a bit of time together then. That's good, because I've got something to show you.'

She drove the car a few streets away and then pulled over. She had spent the morning reading through Billy's diaries. She clicked off the engine and the windscreen wipers stopped. It suddenly felt very quiet.

'This morning I found these hidden in Billy's room. It looks like he has kept diaries over the last five years. Since you've been living with Jeff. I only took a few and they date from different times during that period. This is the most recent one. I know I should have asked you before taking them . . . but once I saw what they were about I thought I couldn't ask you about them in front of Jeff. Here, take a look.'

Chorley watched closely as Grace read through the diary, silently turning from one page to another. All was quiet except for the sound of the rain on the roof of the car. Chorley recognized the last entry in the book as Grace read it. When eventually she looked up at the sergeant, Grace's eyes were full of tears.

30th October

Tonight is the night I have to go.

I just can't take any more.

I don't want to leave her here with him but I have to get away. I just can't stand it anymore. There's another argument starting downstairs and I think I'll go crazy if I have to hear it all again.

I am tired of having to tiptoe around.

Of trying to be silent.

I am tired of not knowing what to say and of not being able to tell anyone what's going on.

I'm tired of trying to be invisible

I'm scared.

Nothing I do helps. I can't make it stop.

It never stops.

*The one person who will understand, the one person
who will know exactly how I feel is Mum. I want her to
cuddle me like she did when I was small and tell me
that it'll be alright and that we can go somewhere
and find a way to be just us two again. To be safe.
But she can't. She's trapped. She's scared too.
But I can go.*

*Not forever. But I can't come back till things
have changed.*

Till then I am disappearing.

'That's a sensitive and intelligent boy you have there.'

Grace nodded slightly as she stared at the diary, her hand trembling.

'Grace, I think I understand what's happening at home and why Billy ran away. Do you think you could tell me what's going on?'

Grace didn't move.

'Grace,' asked Chorley, 'are you safe at home?'

'Yes, of course,' Grace answered, her eyes watching the rain on the windscreen.

Chorley tried again.

'Are you scared at home?'

There was a long silence while they both listened to the rain.

'Grace, do you think Billy is scared to be at home?'

With tears rolling down her face Grace slowly nodded.

'Okay,' Chorley said, 'I'm assuming that what's in Billy's diaries is true. I'd like to know how things are from your point of view.' She leant over and pulled her iPad from her bag. 'I'm going to ask you a list of questions and then I'm going to tell you what we can do to help.'

The two women sat in the parked car by the side of the road in the rain while Grace answered yes or no to Chorley's questions.

It was a while before the sergeant flicked the indicator and pulled away from the kerb and as she did so she began to explain everything to Grace.

Chapter Twenty-Eight

Billy and the old man worked on through the rain, the old man clearing round the headstones in the centre of the graveyard, while Billy worked his way through the tangle of brambles and ivy along the back wall. In some places the undergrowth was so thick that it hid the stones beneath completely. Billy snipped at the barbed strands of the blackberry bushes and tugged at tendrils of ivy, cutting away at the thicker roots on his hands and knees.

He uncovered headstones that were so old it was impossible to read the inscriptions – the letters were worn away or the stone was discoloured and stained by lichen. But on some Billy could pull away the ivy to reveal the words beneath.

Here lies Elizabeth Palmer
1894–1923
And her infant daughter
Penelope
who fell asleep
Aged three days

Albert Draper
1894–1962
and also his wife
Eileen Draper
1905–1985
Reunited

Each stone was a story. Billy tried to imagine who these people had been. What had their lives been like? How had they lived? Had they been kind? Important? Rich? Poor? What had happened to their wives, husbands, children after their deaths? What had the old man said that morning? *Edith never got over the loss.* And her son hadn't even died, just gone, but still she had never recovered from the sadness. He tried not to think about what his own mum was feeling, or what she was doing, but it was hard when each headstone he revealed was another monument to loss and grief.

Occasionally the old man would come along with his wheelbarrow and load up the piles of greenery Billy had cut away and make comments such as 'You're doing a grand job there, lad,' or, 'Keep going! We're nearly there'. Sometimes he would stay for longer and pour a cup of steaming sweet tea from a flask and the two would stand there in the drizzle, passing the cup between them while he told Billy stories about the people on the gravestones. 'Ah, Gilbert. He was a good chap. Bit of trouble, he was, when he was younger, too ready with his fists after a jar or two, but he fell for Betty good and proper and would do anything for her. Meek as a lamb, he was, after they got wed.' Then he would pick up his wheelbarrow and trundle off to another set of head-stones to clear.

It was almost dusk when Billy found the poet's grave. It stood against the wall of the graveyard. It read, *Here lies Frances Cornford, born 1886, died 1960.* And beneath it was carved a poem.

My love came back to me
Under the November tree
Shelterless and dim.
He put his hand upon my shoulder,
He did not think me strange or older,
Nor I, him.

Frances Crofts Cornford née Darwin
1886–1960

Billy stood back and read it. Then he read it again.

'I thought the old man said I would understand what we were doing all this for when I found the poet's grave,' grumbled Billy to himself. 'This doesn't make sense. It doesn't tell me anything.'

He looked around in the gloom for the old man. Where he had been working was cleared and a collection of monuments and stones made dark shapes against the grey evening light but the man himself had gone.

Chapter Twenty-Nine

1st November, local news, 4 p.m.

'Concerns are growing for the safety of a thirteen-year-old boy, Billy McKenna, who has not been seen since leaving school two days ago. This afternoon his mother made an appeal for Billy to return home and asked for assistance from the local community to help find her son.'

'My Billy is a quiet, sensitive and thoughtful boy and it is completely out of character for him to go missing. He is my world and I need him home. To Billy I say this: Billy, I love you. I understand why you went and I want you to know that things will be different when you come home. Get in touch. You're not in any trouble. Please, Billy, let me know you are okay.'

'The search for Billy is being led by Sergeant Chorley of the Brighthaven Constabulary.

She made the following appeal . . .'

'Billy was last seen two days ago, on the thirtieth October, when he left school. At this point we don't believe there's anything suspicious about Billy's disappearance but we have no information on where he is now or where he may be heading. There have not been any sightings of Billy. He is not in any trouble, but, as you can imagine, we are concerned that he is out on the streets. Alone. We are hoping that Billy is still in the local area and appeal to the public to check their sheds and garages and to get in touch if they think they may have seen Billy. We are trying to get a picture of his movements on the evening of thirtieth October and ask people living in the Bransden area of the city to check their CCTV or dashcams and contact us with any relevant information. If you think you have seen Billy or spoken to Billy, please get in touch. Call us, contact us on social media or drop into any police station. We rely on information we receive from the public to help in cases like this. Please know that we are grateful for any assistance you can give us.'

CHAPTER THIRTY

Izzie left her bike propped up against the chapel wall and, guided by her phone light, went to find Billy. Before she got to the pillbox she found him forking leaves and branches out of a wheelbarrow and on to the compost heap in the corner of the graveyard.

'What are you doing *that* for? Are you lame or what? Isn't that someone else's job? And why are you doing it now? It *is* dark, you know.'

'Well, maybe *you* shouldn't go creeping up on people in graveyards!' said Billy. 'What are you doing here anyway?'

'I came to see if you were all right. It's not every day that the boy you sit next to in maths takes to hiding out in a graveyard, you know. So . . . what *are* you doing?'

'I've been helping out this old man who works here. Just to pass the time. I'm clearing up before I go to bed.'

'Okaaay . . .' Izzie replied. 'You're in a graveyard doing stuff for some random old bloke? That doesn't sound weird at all! Sounds *great*. Really! Luckily, alongside checking that you haven't died of pneumonia, I also came here to bring you these.' She pulled some crisps from her pocket. 'And these.' Followed by a multipack of chocolate bars. 'Oh, and to show you this . . .'

Izzie pulled her phone from her pocket and clicked on a link. The video clip of Billy's mum began to play . . .

'My Billy is a quiet, sensitive and thoughtful boy and it is completely out of character for him to go missing. He is my world and I need him home . . .'

Billy was mesmerized by the sight of his mum there on that tiny screen.

She looked *so* tired, *so* pale and *so* small between Jeff on one side and the policewoman on the other. The ache to see her felt like a pain in his chest.

'So you are hiding here and you've asked *me* to keep it secret. And now EVERYONE knows you're missing,' Izzie was saying. 'You do know I could get in *massive* trouble for this, don't you?'

'Er . . . yeah. Sorry, Izzie. I didn't ask to be found, you know. I didn't . . . It's just that . . .' He looked hopelessly at her, both their faces lit in the gloom by the phone screen. 'Can you just play that again?'

Izzie pressed play . . .

'My Billy is a quiet, sensitive and thoughtful boy . . .'

Billy watched and this time he noticed something he hadn't seen the first time.

'Izzie, can you play it *again*?'

She huffed, but pressed play.

And there it was.

Such a small movement.

Billy's mother spoke, looking directly at the camera. In one hand she had her notes, which were written on a piece of paper that was tucked inside an A6 notebook.

Billy gasped as he recognized it as one of his own diaries. Grace's other hand was under Jeff's hand on the tabletop. But as she said 'things will be different when you come home' she slid her hand out from under Jeff's. He saw Jeff's sideways glance, so slight that it was little more than a twitch, but Billy's mother continued to speak directly to the camera.

'Look at that!' cried Billy.

Izzie played it again. It was definitely there – that movement away from Jeff at the exact moment that she said 'things will be different'. She had one of his diaries. Was this a signal, a message within a message, just for Billy? Possibilities rushed through his mind as he stared at his mother paused on Izzie's phone screen.

'What are you on about? This is *serious*. I'm showing you this because that policewoman there, on that screen next to *your* mum, is *my* mum! I can tell you that they don't usually do this unless they think a kid has been kidnapped or something. And you haven't even been gone for very long. You're going to be in the papers and on the national news. You know what this means, don't you? EVERYONE will be looking out for you now. EVERYONE.

'*Everyone* will be worried about you. And *I* am lying to all those people . . . and my mum. I *HAVE* to tell them you're here!'

'But you *promised* . . .'

'Actually, I didn't. You *HAVE* to go home!'
'Izzie, I can't. I need to know it'll be different, not just hope it will.'

'Different from what? Just *what* is
your *PROBLEM*?'

'I'll tell you if you promise not to give me up for a bit
longer. Just keep my secret for one more day. *Please?*'

'Okay. But this had better be good,' grumbled Izzie. '*You*
might not mind being in trouble but *I* do!'

They sat side by side on a bench in the dark and Billy was
glad to not be able to see Izzie's face as he started to talk . . .
He explained how it had just been the two of them – him
and his mum. Then Jeff came along. And how he had
been great fun and how happy his mum had been.
And then the gradual changes. So slight you
could hardly spot them. But that
his mum had disappeared.

She'd been in the same body, the same clothes, but her sparkle had gradually ebbed away until she just wasn't her any more.

And then he talked about the violence. How he couldn't bear to hear it, see it or feel it any more. He just had to disappear.

'Only you and that old bloke know I'm here, Izzie. He's promised not to tell. Can't you too? You can protect me from having to go back.'

'Oh, Billy. I'm so sorry.' Izzie reached out and awkwardly put a hand on Billy's arm. 'I can't believe you didn't say anything. It must be horrible for you. Now I totally get why you're here. I *will* keep your secret, but only for one more day. You know, it's not just me and that old guy who knows you're here? There's some Year 11 girl going round saying she was saved by a "ghost" in this graveyard on Halloween. Was that you?'

Billy shrugged and nodded.

'Don't you think people might begin to put two and two together? One more day, Billy – you can't just stay here forever. They'll come and find you, Billy McKenna, and then you'll *have* to go home.'

Billy watched Izzie's bike light wobble away in the dark. He stood alone among the stones, listening to the whoosh of the trees in the breeze above his head and the hum of a distant road. He breathed in the night air and felt his heart slow. Izzie was right. His time here was running out. He needed to think. To decide what to do.

Steadily he walked back to the pillbox, playing the image of his mum pulling her hand away from under Jeff's over and over in his mind. 'Things will be different,' she had said. But how?

When he got to the doorway of the pillbox there was something resting against the ivy that covered the entrance. It was a metal flask of food wrapped in a cloth to keep it warm.

CHAPTER THIRTY-ONE

1st November, Sergeant Chorley's car,
Brownsfield Close, 9 p.m.

Sergeant Chorley clicked send on the message to her daughter and turned back to Grace whose phone buzzed again with another call. It seemed that Grace's phone was always ringing or pinging with messages. Yet she apparently didn't have any friends.

'Is that Jeff *again*?' asked Chorley. 'Is it like this all the time?'

The phone buzzed once more.

'No. Well, yes . . . I don't know. He's just worried about me, you know?'

'Grace, given some of the things we now know about Jeff, do you really think that's true?'

'No. I suppose not. Not really,' Grace said quietly. 'But it's just hard to talk about . . .'

'I can understand that. And you talking us through some of the things that Billy has recorded in his diary has been really valuable. Anything you can share to help us build up a picture of how Jeff behaves makes our case against him stronger. I know it's difficult, Grace, but it will help us to protect you. And Billy.'

The phone buzzed again.

'Okay. Yes. It *is* like this all the time unless we're together. Yes. He wants to know where I am, who I am with and what I am doing.'

'How did it get to this point, do you think, Grace?'

'I don't know really. At first I thought it was sweet that he cared about whether I was all right when I was out, you know?' Grace looked nervously towards the house, where Jeff was pacing the sitting room like a caged animal, his phone in his hand. 'But then it got that he was ringing and texting me non-stop and he said he worried that something had happened to me if I didn't reply straight away.

He seemed really concerned, you know? It upset him so much.'

Grace's phone buzzed again.

'And then . . . I don't know . . . bit by bit I just stopped doing things that I thought would worry him, like going to the cinema when my phone had to be off. I almost didn't realize I was doing it. I just didn't want to upset him, you know? In the end I just stopped going out, unless it was to work, or to the supermarket. It just made life easier.'

'One of the entries in Billy's diaries was about Jeff coming to find you in the supermarket? Does that happen often?'

'Poor Billy. All this time I thought I was shielding him from the worst of it. But he's noticed everything. Yes. Sometimes Jeff would surprise us, you know? He would arrive at the supermarket or at my work or at the school gate when I was picking up Billy when he was younger. Sometimes he would sit in the car and watch to see who I spoke to. He gets really jealous, you know?'

The two women sat and watched Jeff pace back and forth in the rectangle of window overlooking the street.

'I thought that I was making a better life for me and Billy. But I've trapped us. And now I've lost Billy too.'

'*You* haven't done anything wrong, Grace. What Jeff has done to you and Billy is a crime. D'you understand? You are so brave to talk about it and we'll do everything we can to help you and Billy.'

Grace smiled weakly at the policewoman.

'Your amazing son has given us a record of more than a hundred instances of domestic abuse. Our priority is keeping you safe and making sure Billy is safe too. But first we have to make sure that he comes home.'

Grace and Sergeant Chorley stepped out of the car, walked down the cul-de-sac, crossed the road and went up the garden path together. The door opened as Grace reached for the lock with her key.

'You've been a long time! Is everything okay?' Jeff smiled as his eyes darted from one woman to the other. 'I've been worried. You weren't answering your phone.'

'Ah! That was my fault, Mr Lansdale. Grace has been helping us piece together some of the places that Billy used to like visiting as a small child. We're already having a good response to the TV appeal and we're hoping to get some firm information on sightings of Billy. Hopefully I'll be back in the morning with any new information that comes up. Until then I can assure you that our night shift are working hard on the case. Finding Billy is a priority for us . . .'

Jeff stood close behind Grace as they watched Chorley walk away.

'You didn't answer my calls.'

His voice was gruff.

'I couldn't, could I? I was answering questions about Billy. You knew where I was. You left me at the police station earlier . . .'

Grace eased out of her jacket and hung it on the peg. 'No news here, I suppose?' She kept her voice light, afraid that Jeff would know what she had really been talking about.

'No. Nothing. I'll teach that boy a lesson when he gets home. Putting us through all this worry. I'm on an early shift tomorrow so I'm off to bed.' He turned and began to climb the stairs. 'Oh, and there's another bowl of something from that busybody down the street and she brought a load of cards with her. They're on the kitchen table.'

Grace watched him until he turned on to the landing and out of sight. She felt icy cold. How could she ever have believed this man loved her and Billy?

She walked through to the kitchen. There was a casserole dish with a folded piece of paper sellotaped to the top. Opening it, she saw a black-and-white photocopied photo of Billy staring out at her, with HELP FIND BILLY underneath it. There was a Facebook address and a message asking for volunteers to come forward. In handwriting underneath was a note.

Thought you'd like to see the poster we've made.
Had a great response already and I've been
collecting cards from some well-wishers.
Chicken stew for you. Love Lorraine

Next to the casserole dish was a pile of cards and notes on the table. Grace reached for the first one.

So sorry to see on the news that your son has gone
missing. Do call if you think we can help with
anything. Pat and Tracy (79 Ballingdon Street)

Grace had no idea who Pat and Tracy were, but it was kind of them to send a message. She picked up another.

To Billy's parents, we're thinking of you at this difficult time, John, Jenny, Toby and Ella

And another:

Let me know if I can help! Suzie

Suzie! Grace had forgotten about the envelope from this morning. It seemed so long ago. She went to the hall and reached into her jacket pocket. There it was. Inside the envelope was a neatly folded piece of A4 paper. On it was the name of a website and a printout of information about seeking safety. And below was a handwritten note. It said:

I think I understand what is happening to you.
I am here to help if you need it.
I think you should have an emergency bag packed.
Here is a list of what should be in it . . .

Grace read it again.

Then she opened the kitchen door enough to check that she could hear snoring coming from upstairs.

She reached for a backpack from the cupboard under the stairs and very quietly she began to fill it.

CHAPTER THIRTY-TWO

It was only just becoming light when Billy heard car tyres crunching on the gravel.

Was this it? Had Izzie not kept her word after all? Or the old man perhaps?

He scrambled out of his sleeping bag and stumbled to the window.

A car door slammed.

Billy's heart pounded.

He dipped to the other window to see if he could see
anything but Billy's view was limited. He strained to see
who was there, who was coming for him.

And then he saw.

He was tall and thin and wrapped in a big black coat. He
walked hesitantly, as if he was trying to find his bearings.
To find his way around.

He looked as if he was searching for something.

But the man only seemed to be interested in the graves. He peered intently at them, reading the names on each headstone before moving on to the next one. Billy watched him go steadily through the graveyard until he stopped on the furthest side from the pillbox, directly in Billy's line of vision.

The man stood there with such a sad look on his face. He raked his hand through his curls and across his eyes as if he was weary. And then he clamped his hand over his mouth and Billy realized that the man was crying. Slow steady tears rolled down his cheeks as he gazed at a headstone.

I should feel ashamed to be standing here, spying on a stranger's grief, thought Billy as his heart slowed.

But he couldn't draw back from watching the man. He thought of all the times when he was younger that Jeff had said, 'Man up, Billy. Men don't cry!

Get some bloody backbone, can't you? You're an embarrassment!' and of Jeff's cocky, pushy idea of manhood. But here was this man with a beautiful face, openly weeping.

Billy watched as the man stood in the quiet of the graveyard. After a while he dried his eyes and turned and walked away. A few moments later Billy heard the car door slam shut and the car drive slowly back down All Souls' Lane.

He let out a long sigh of relief.

His secret was safe for the time being at least.

Chapter Thirty-Three

2nd November, 24 Brownsfield Close, 8 a.m.

Grace had been too anxious to sleep. She was staring out at the street when the two police cars pulled up outside. Was it news about Billy? Chorley hadn't mentioned anything. Surely she would have called if she had any news? Maybe it was bad news and she wanted to tell Grace face to face?

Grace couldn't move.

She couldn't get up from her chair as she watched three police officers get out of one car and two out of another. People further down the street opened their doors and stared.

Oh god, let Billy be okay.

Please.

They walked up the path – shapes of black and high-vis yellow. One stayed at the front gate. Lorraine was standing in her drive.

Please let Billy be okay.

They knocked on the door and the sound reverberated around the house. One of the constables stared directly at her through the window but Grace still couldn't move. She heard heavy thuds down the stairs and the catch unlocked as Jeff opened the door.

'Mr Lansdale? Jeff Lansdale?' asked the police constable calmly.

'Yes? How can I help? Do you have news about Billy?'

'Mr Lansdale, I am arresting you under the Serious Crime Act of 2015. You do not have to say anything. But it may harm your defence if you do not mention when questioned, something that you later rely on in court.

Anything you do say may be given in evidence.' The constable reached out and clipped a handcuff round Jeff's wrist.

'What? I've got nothing to do with Billy going off! This is a mistake! This is a bloody outrage!'

'This is not about Billy, Mr Lansdale. You are being arrested for years of suspected domestic abuse of your partner, Grace McKenna.'

In the street the neighbours had their phones out and filmed as Jeff was bundled into one of the police cars and as it turned and drove slowly out of Brownsfield Close.

Grace hadn't moved. It was as if she had watched it all on a TV screen. She couldn't believe what she'd seen. It didn't feel real at all. But it was real. She was shaking all over. A young police constable stepped into the room.

'Grace? My colleague here is going to make you a cup of tea. And then we're going to talk through some of your options with you.'

CHAPTER THIRTY-FOUR

The old man arrived later than usual that morning. When he did he was wearing a red silk neckerchief and carrying a wicker hamper and a pile of blankets.

'You look smart,' said Billy as the man unpacked a foil-wrapped bacon sandwich from the hamper and handed it to him.

'Well, my lad, tonight's the night! *This* is what we've been working for. Still a bit of tidying to do but we should get it all done on time.'

He rubbed his hands together eagerly.

'I still don't get it,' mumbled Billy between mouthfuls. 'I don't understand why we're doing all this or what it's got to do with that poem. Is there gonna be some kind of

memorial to that poet or something? Because I'd rather make myself scarce when people start arriving, if that's the case.'

The old man grinned.

'You still don't know what today is then? Don't worry. You'll see. And you needn't worry about the guests. I promise you they won't say a word. Now, we still need to clean a couple of the statues and there's still a lot of weeds over Reverend Caldwell over there. You can do the grubby stuff, I don't want to spoil me glad rags. I'm just going to rake up the leaves and get a bonfire going and then I'll join you.'

Billy finished his sandwich and watched as his companion walked off across the graveyard to get the wheelbarrow from beside the chapel wall. There was a spring in the old man's step. He was clearly excited. Whatever was going to happen seemed to be making him pretty happy.

Chapter Thirty-Five

2nd November, 24 Brownsfield Close, 12 noon

Grace clicked the door shut and stood at the sitting-room window. She waved goodbye to the police car as it pulled away from the kerb. She watched it until she could see it no more and then stood looking out at Brownsfield Close.

She put the kettle on and made another cup of tea. Each sound seemed too loud against the quiet of the house. She walked from one room to another with her mug. In her mind's eye she remembered how it used to be when it was just her and Billy in their own flat – a bit chaotic, but cosy. Magazines and books, her basket of knitting, Billy's drawings on the mantelpiece, his toys in the tub by the sofa and everywhere else for that matter! Now? Now it looked like a show home. There was no evidence that she and Billy lived here. There was one photo of her and Jeff on the side-board but Billy was nowhere to be seen. How had it happened? It was almost as if he had been erased from his own home long before he had left. How could she not have noticed? Grace picked up the picture of her and Jeff and dropped it into the kitchen bin.

Then she went upstairs to the room she shared with Jeff. She stripped the bed and took Jeff's pillow. She bundled the sheets and duvet cover into the washing machine and took the pillow outside and shoved it in the rubbish. With fresh bedding she remade the bed, putting her own pillow in the middle of the clean white sheet. She looked around the room and her eyes rested on the wardrobe. On her knees she pulled out boxes of shoes, and there, at the back, she felt the tin.

And there they were. One picture after another of her life with Billy before Jeff. Photos of Billy as a baby, snuggled up in her arms. The nursery outing in a raincoat that was too big for him, rolled up at the sleeves. Yellow wellies. Big grin with tiny teeth. Their camping holiday in the leaky tent. School photos with that tuft of hair that would never stick down. And the drawings by Billy – pictures of them both with spiky fingers, round eyes and scribbled hair. The later ones of carefully coloured squares spelling out the letters for MUMMY on graph paper or a heart coloured in with felt-tip pens. She took them all downstairs.

With another mug of tea Grace spread the pictures out and began to prop them up around the room, tucking them into the edge of picture frames and lining them up along the mantelpiece. With each one a set of memories came tumbling back. Grace felt sad and happy at the same time.

Come home, Billy. Come home.

Her fingers worked faster, rummaging through the tin and putting the pictures, one after another after another, around the room. Then she stopped at one photo. It was of the two of them in the park. How long ago? Ten years? Eleven? They had taken a picnic to sit by the lake but the ducks had come and pecked away at their sandwiches. Billy had laughed, rolling about on the ground, ducks hopping around him to get at his crisps. They had giggled so much that she couldn't hold the camera still and a passer-by had snapped it for her. Grace and Billy rosy-cheeked from laughing, wide grins, her hair dishevelled and catching the light.

Grace took the photo upstairs and into Billy's room. She laid it on his folded pyjamas and sat on the bed, looking around. Everything was in order. Neat and tidy.

Come home, Billy. Come home.

The doorbell rang.

Grace jumped.

Was it Billy?

The press?

One of the neighbours?

Jeff?

As she walked down the stairs she saw the tall slim shape through the frosted glass of the front door. Not Billy then. Her heart sank. She opened the door a fraction and peeped through the gap – chain still on.

There stood a tall, thin man in a long dark coat. He had a long woollen scarf wrapped round his neck, dark curls and twinkling blue eyes.

'Hello, Grace!' he said.

Chapter Thirty-Six

They worked all day. The old man seemed in good humour and whistled as he went back and forth with his barrow, raking leaves and picking up the stray branches and brambles that Billy cleared from the few remaining overgrown headstones. By mid-afternoon Billy had done all he thought he could find to do. He stood back and surveyed the graveyard.

The transformation was remarkable. Where there had been long grass, nettles, bindweed and brambles with only the occasional stone peeping through, there were now clear spaces round each headstone, the variety of shapes clear to see in contrast to the walkways between them. Surely they were done? He found the old man poking at a pile of burning leaves.

'I think we've done it all. This place is as cleaned up as it can be, I reckon.'

The old man straightened and looked at Billy, his eyes watery from the smoke. 'Oh, aye? Grand. Then maybe you can just finish off by filling that bucket by the tap and giving that old angel a bit of a clean-up?'

Billy found the bucket. It had a brush in it and a cloth draped over the side. He splashed water into it from the tap in the wall. Although there was more than one angel statue in the graveyard, he knew which one the old man meant and set his bucket under the stone carving he had been looking at the first time they had spoken.

He raised the brush and started scrubbing at the green mould on her hair. Streams of greeny-brown water began to run down the stonework. He wet the brush and scrubbed some more and the honey-coloured stone began to show through. Billy cleaned in small, circular movements, rinsing as he went. He worked all down the angel – her hair, wings, hands, the pillar she leant against. But he left her face until last.

Refilling his bucket with clean water, he took the cloth and looked up into the angel's face. With gentle movements he brushed away the grime and with the cloth he wiped away the dark stains from under her eyes. He thought of all the times his mother had washed his face when he was small, just like this. The memory was like a sharp pain. He rinsed out the cloth again and wiped her face once more and stood back.

There was no beam of sunlight this time and the yellow stone was dark where the angel was still wet. But still she looked better. And stronger. Billy looked more closely.

Washing away dirt, mould and lichen had revealed a slight frown to the angel's face. She seemed to be concentrating or determined. It reminded him of his mother's expression as she looked into the camera in that police appeal. *'Things will be different when you come home.'*

She *had* been determined. But what could she *do*? How could his mum make things different for them both? She had been powerless for so long. They both had. What could she do and how would Billy know?

He loved his mum so much.

But he couldn't go home until he knew it was safe. And he knew he was running out of time.

The old man and Izzie had said they would keep his secret only until today.

Maybe in the morning it would be time to move on. Another hideaway, perhaps.

Chapter Thirty-Seven

2nd November, 24 Brownsfield Close, 5 p.m.

'I'm so sorry, Grace.'

The man sat at the kitchen table, photos of Billy scattered before him.

'That's not good enough! Look at him! Look!' Grace stabbed at the table with her finger. 'It was me who got up with him night after night when he was teething. Me who had to take days off from work when he was poorly. It was me who couldn't get a well-paid job because I had to care for him on my own! And now, now that he's GONE you come here asking about him!'

'I know how it must look, Grace. I had no idea until I saw

you on the news. I did the maths and thought it might be possible that he was my son. But even if he isn't, I wanted to come and offer my help.'

'It's too late! You're thirteen years too late! How could you have left like that? A few postcards and then NOTHING! You just disappeared! You left me no choice but to cope on my own! After everything we had you evaporated into thin air!'

'I'm so sorry, Grace. I never meant it to happen. I didn't think it through. I wanted to get away; I could only think about myself. I was selfish and young. We were both so young! I never wanted to hurt you! I just thought I would go away for a while, see a bit of the world – and that I would come back and we would pick up where we left off. But I drifted and didn't keep in touch and then, when I wanted to come back, I was too ashamed of how I had treated you. Just going off like that. I figured you'd never have me back. That you'd have moved on . . . And then I saw you on the news. Please let me try to make it up to you. Please let me help you find Billy. Tell me what can I do?'

'Nothing! I've managed without you so far. I'm sure I can manage without you now.'

'Please let me help, Grace! I am so lost. I don't know what to do for the best.'

One look at Grace's furious expression silenced him.

'*You* feel lost?' Grace whispered back at him, her voice quavering with fury. 'You stand here talking about yourself! When you disappeared I lost you. I lost my youth. I lost hope. I lost my family. I lost my friends. Billy has been the only good thing in my life and now he is gone. And you come here and talk about losing yourself? I don't want to hear it! I don't want to see you.'

He raked a hand through his hair. 'Look, here's my number. Call me if you think of anything I can do. Grace, I really want to help. I really am so, so sorry.'

Grace sat and stared at the table, snapshots of Billy grinning up at her, as the man let himself out of the front door.

It clicked shut behind him and all was quiet again.

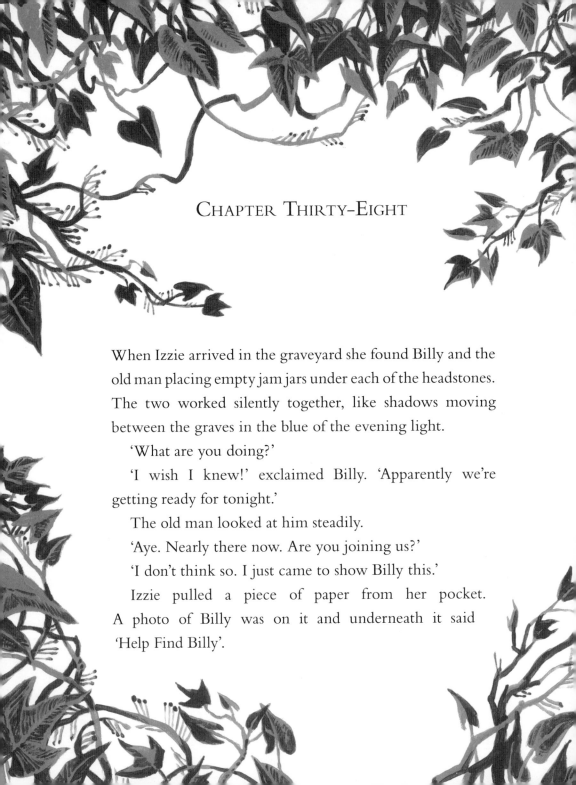

Chapter Thirty-Eight

When Izzie arrived in the graveyard she found Billy and the old man placing empty jam jars under each of the headstones. The two worked silently together, like shadows moving between the graves in the blue of the evening light.

'What are you doing?'

'I wish I knew!' exclaimed Billy. 'Apparently we're getting ready for tonight.'

The old man looked at him steadily.

'Aye. Nearly there now. Are you joining us?'

'I don't think so. I just came to show Billy this.'

Izzie pulled a piece of paper from her pocket. A photo of Billy was on it and underneath it said 'Help Find Billy'.

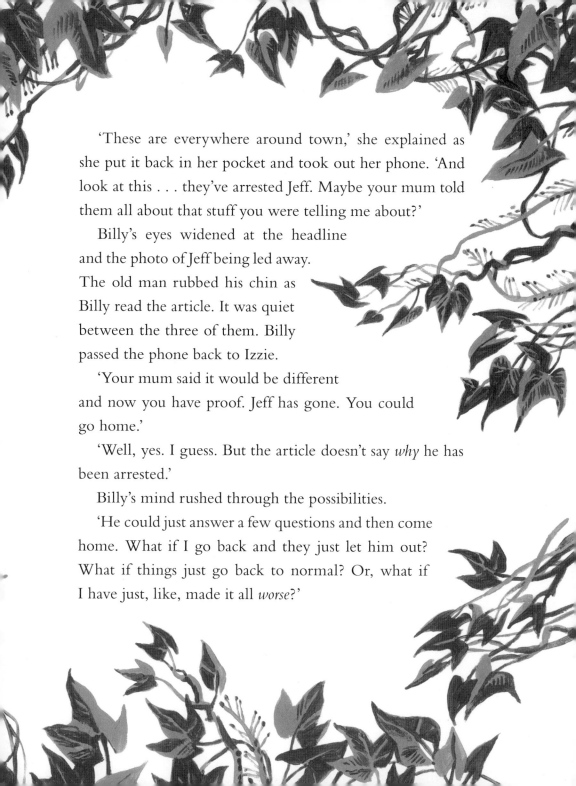

'These are everywhere around town,' she explained as she put it back in her pocket and took out her phone. 'And look at this . . . they've arrested Jeff. Maybe your mum told them all about that stuff you were telling me about?'

Billy's eyes widened at the headline and the photo of Jeff being led away. The old man rubbed his chin as Billy read the article. It was quiet between the three of them. Billy passed the phone back to Izzie.

'Your mum said it would be different and now you have proof. Jeff has gone. You could go home.'

'Well, yes. I guess. But the article doesn't say *why* he has been arrested.'

Billy's mind rushed through the possibilities.

'He could just answer a few questions and then come home. What if I go back and they just let him out? What if things just go back to normal? Or, what if I have just, like, made it all *worse*?'

The words tumbled out. Instead of feeling relief he imagined Jeff's anger at having been arrested. He thought of Jeff arriving back at the house, bristling with rage, spittle flying from his lips as he blamed Billy, blamed his mum for the humiliation of being taken away by the police in front of the neighbours. He imagined Jeff crashing through the house, fists clenched, knuckles white. The fear rushed through him. Billy bit his bottom lip to stop it trembling.

'But your mum must have done or said something!' Izzie was saying. 'They've taken him away! *Surely* you'll be safe now.'

Billy imagined Jeff blocking his mother into a corner.

'You *could* at least call her and let her know you're all right.'

'I don't think I can. Not tonight,' Billy whispered.

'What? That's just cruel! Why wouldn't you? She must be worried sick!' Izzie's voice was rising.

Billy couldn't say that he simply didn't feel strong enough.

If he spoke to his mum, he knew this safe time, this safe place, would be over. He had such a longing to see her.

He wanted to hear her voice. He wanted a hug. But he was so afraid. Afraid of Jeff. Afraid that nothing would change.

He knew he was staring at Izzie open-mouthed, but no words came.

'You're here preparing for some *party* and your mum's alone! And you don't give a—'

'I *do* care, it's just . . .'

'I don't want to hear it, Billy McKenna! That's it. I'm done. I felt sorry for you. I actually liked you. I *really* liked you! But now I see you're just bloody selfish! I said I would give you another day and I have. *You* haven't kept your side of the deal. I've had it with you. With all of this.'

And Izzie turned her back on Billy and the old man and stomped out of sight.

Billy watched her go.

He tried to swallow down a sob.

The old man looked at Billy and Izzie, and then followed Izzie to where she was trying to unlock her bike.

From where he stood Billy couldn't hear what was being said between them but he could clearly see Izzie angrily gesturing over to Billy and the old man trying to steady and calm her. He was leaning towards Izzie, his hands together as if he was pleading with her. They both turned and looked across at Billy, the old man still talking.

Izzie took a doubtful look back at him, shrugged, pulled at her bike and walked off into the evening gloom.

The old man steadily made his way back to Billy. He reached out and awkwardly placed a rough hand on Billy's shoulder.

'I think I've persuaded her to keep quiet for tonight but I can't be sure. She's strong-minded, that one, and a good friend to you whatever cross words she's just said. And she's got a point, lad. She'll be thinking of your ma just like you are but without knowin' what you know and havin' seen what you've seen, whatever that is. I can see in your face you've got your reasons. C'mon, now, let's set to. Like I said to your friend, I'll wager you'll feel differently once you've seen what happens here tonight.'

Chapter Thirty-Nine

2nd November, 76 Highsett, 9 p.m.

Izzie Chorley took a deep breath and called her mum's number again. Every time the call wasn't answered her resolve ebbed further. The old man's words kept repeating in her mind.

A little more time . . . a little understanding . . . it'll all be clearer in the morning . . . I'm lookin' out for him. He's safe for now. I won't let any harm come to him.

Maybe she was being rash? Maybe she should give Billy and that peculiar old bloke the benefit of the doubt. What difference would one more night really make? Billy seemed safe enough.

Izzie was hesitating as she wondered if she should hang up when the call was answered.

'Izzie? What is it?' Her mum's voice was distracted. 'Hang on . . .' The phone was slightly muffled as her mum said, 'The file is on my desk. And mine was the latte. Ta. I'll be there in two ticks.' And then clear again. 'Izzie. Sorry, love. What is it? I've got a lot on . . .'

'I know, Mum. Sorry. I just wanted to talk to you.'

Izzie heard her mum's sigh. 'No. It's the blue folder . . . the other blue! Hang on, Izzie.' The phone was put down and as Izzie waited she recalled other things the old man had said . . .

He needs to do it in his own way and in his own time . . . We need to be patient with him.

Then it was her mum's voice in her ear again. 'What about, Izzie? I'll be home soon. Can it wait?'

'I don't know. There is something I need to tell you.'

'Hang on!' The phone was muffled again. 'Just give me a mo. I'll just finish this call, then I'll come through to your office. Right. Izzie. What is it you wanted?'

'I didn't want anything. Just to tell you something.'

'Gawd! I've just spilt my bloody coffee. Was it about school? Can it wait? I'll be home soon. Can we talk then? You can tell me about your day later, okay?'

'But . . .'

'Please, Izzie. I'm sure it can wait. I'll be home soon. Pop a pizza in the oven. I'll be able to give you proper time when I'm home, sweetheart, okay? Love you!' And the phone clicked off.

Izzie stood in the quiet of the kitchen staring at her mobile. Then she walked to the freezer, took out a pizza, put it on a tray and into the cooker. She stared at the light of the oven, watching the cheese slowly melt. Wondering.

After a while she pulled the brown-edged pizza from the tray, cut off a slice and, with a plate in one hand, the poster about Billy and her phone in her free hand, she walked up to her room.

As she looked out of her bedroom window she imagined Grace alone at home, Billy in the graveyard, her mum busy at work. She just couldn't work out what she should do.

Maybe the old bloke was right, Izzie thought as she pulled on her pyjamas.

It'll all be clearer in the morning . . .

CHAPTER FORTY

'So . . . we just sit here like this? This is it?'

'Yep,' said the old man. 'We just wait.'

Billy looked out over the graveyard. Candle flames flickered by every headstone. A cold wind blew around them and rushed through the trees above their heads as the

two of them sat on the bench wrapped in blankets.
The old man passed a cup of tea from his flask.

'And is it only us? All this work and this "event"
is just the two of us? No one else is coming?'

'Yep.'

'Isn't that a bit . . . *odd*? This isn't going to be some
spooky ritual or something, is it?'

'Nope,' said the old man, his eyes fixed straight ahead
on the candlelight dancing on the headstones. 'It'll be
a night you'll never forget but you need to be patient.'

So the two of them sat shivering and listening to
the roar of the wind in the trees.

Waiting.

Chapter Forty-One

2nd November, 24 Brownsfield Close, 10.30 p.m.

Grace put down what she was doing and went to answer the door. Lorraine stood there on the path in her slippers, her cardie wrapped about her.

'Hello, love,' she said. 'I just thought I'd pop round. I know it's late but I saw your light on and thought I'd just check in.'

Grace opened the door wider. 'Have you heard anything, you know, from Facebook, about Billy? Has anyone seen him?'

'Sorry, pet. Not yet. Nothing concrete. But I've had so many volunteers signing up, especially with you being on the news with that appeal. And that's why I'm here. Now, a little search group of us are going to be looking over at the old industrial estate for your boy tomorrow, unless we get any sightings posted on the Facebook page. We're going to head out there early so we can start as soon as it's light.'

Lorraine looked beyond Grace into the hall and kitchen.

'I saw what happened earlier and thought that you'd be on your own. So, instead of you sitting here worrying why don't I pick you up tomorrow and you come along with us? Young Suzie next door will be coming along too.'

Grace nodded slowly. At least she would be doing something practical to help Billy.

She found herself wrapped in a big warm hug and then Lorraine was gone. Marvelling at the kindness of people, Grace returned to the backpack on the kitchen table. She already had the passports, the bank cards, spare keys, their birth certificates and some cash carefully hidden in the back pockets. She took the bag up to Billy's room and slid open his drawers and took some T-shirts, jeans and a hoody. From his bed she took his neatly folded pyjamas and pushed them all into her bag. She picked up his mobile and the charger and then went into her room.

From the cupboard she took jeans, joggers, a couple of jumpers. She pushed underwear into the side pockets of the backpack and then added toothpaste and toothbrushes from the bathroom.

Downstairs she collected the drawings and photos of Billy from around the house and slipped them into the bag as well.

Then she buried the bag in the back of the cupboard under the stairs so that it would be hidden safely until the morning.

There was no way she would be able to sleep so she went to sit on the sofa and stared out at the street.

And waited.

CHAPTER FORTY-TWO

And then it happened.

The wind dropped and a stillness descended over the graveyard. It became quiet.

The old man put a finger to his lips, staring ahead,
seeking something between the stones.

'Shhh,' he said steadily. 'Look . . .'

The first one they saw was a small child. He came toddling out from behind the gravestones, wobbling as he took unsteady steps. He stopped and looked about him, as if waiting for someone else. An older girl in long skirts, stockings and boots, running to scoop up the toddler, chased by two boys in caps. The three of them looked as if they were laughing and calling but no sound came out as they darted and dashed between the headstones. A woman appeared and caught them up in her arms, hugging them all as if she hadn't seen them for such a long time. Covering them in kisses. The boys broke away and the chase resumed, this time with the woman also dipping behind the stones and trying to catch the children with arms open wide.

Billy watched, open-mouthed, unable to comprehend what he was seeing. The old man nudged him and indicated the other side of the graveyard.

A man, bald on top with long sideburns and tufts of hair sticking out around his ears, stepped out from behind a stone, a book tucked under the arm of his frock coat. He stepped tentatively between the graves until he reached a small headstone, where he stood, as if waiting, rocking gently backwards and forwards on the balls of his feet.

'Is it . . . is that Reverend Caldwell?' whispered Billy, thinking back to cleaning the headstone earlier that day.

And where the small stone stood there was now a woman, kind-eyed and full-cheeked. The reverend looped his arm and the woman slipped hers through his and together they followed the path under the yews, their heads close together as they silently talked.

'That was his housekeeper. They loved each other for years but never spoke of it. So good to see them together.'

The couple passed a bench and on it sat a soldier, his hands cupped round those of his sweetheart, their knees touching. A small boy darted in and out of the trees as a young man in braces strode behind him. Three elderly women sat on headstones close together, knitting and chuckling at some inaudible joke. A young man in uniform swept the fringe from the eyes of his companion and the two leant in, foreheads touching. A young woman, strands of hair drifting from her cap, stood rocking a baby back and forth, gazing into the tiny bundle of blankets. More and more people appeared and soon the graveyard was busy with the shifting shapes of silent people.

'So, what has this got to do with the poet? Is she here?' asked Billy.

'She'll be here somewhere. She's here every year. But this isn't about the poet herself, it's about the poem . . .'

My love came back to me
Under the November tree
Shelterless and dim.
He put his hand upon my shoulder,
He did not think me strange or older,
Nor I, him.

The old man recited the poem that Billy had read on the stone, still staring ahead as if keen not to miss something.

'But I don't get it,' Billy whispered. 'What does it *mean*?'

'Tonight. Today. The second of November. It's All Souls' Night. And we are here in All Souls' graveyard. Each year, on the same day, the souls of the dead are reunited with those they loved most at the time when they were their happiest. Their love for each other is undimmed by time and their joy at being together again . . . Well –' the old man's voice became gruff – 'it pulls at the old heartstrings, doesn't it?'

But Billy couldn't answer. He was transfixed, watching a woman and a boy, arms round each other as they walked and chatted. He looked on as the mother and son passed by the bench, absorbed in conversation. Passing by in the opposite direction were two men, both with large noses and heavy eyebrows, but about thirty years apart in age. Each walked with a strong stride, gesturing as if having an animated conversation.

'Ah! There she is!' sighed the old man. A wide grin spread across his face. From the furthest corner of the graveyard a woman stood by the headstone with the roses on it. She was slightly stooped with a cardigan about her shoulders. She looked shyly about her. 'My own Edith!'

The old man stared as if he was drinking up every detail of her. He leant forward, tears in his eyes, his bottom lip trembling. 'My own girl . . .' he whispered.

Billy gazed as the woman picked her way steadily through the graveyard, looking about her as if seeking someone. Then her eyes rested on the bench and the old man and a smile lit up her face.

Without taking her eyes from him she began to walk towards him. 'My Edith,' the old man was muttering.

And he hobbled off along the pathway, oblivious to the silent families, friends and lovers that weaved about him, his eyes fixed steadily on his wife. Edith looked up at him as he approached and she smiled then reached up and touched his cheek. She linked her arm through his and together they turned to walk round the path that circled the graveyard. Billy watched as they disappeared and reappeared behind the yew trees, the old man gazing and gazing at his wife as if he couldn't get enough of her.

Billy sat in the silence and watched as the figures swept past them or chatted on gravestones. The hours passed as mute people expressed their happiness around him, delighted at being reunited even for a short time.

Billy's heart ached to feel that happiness too. And it ached to see his mum again.

CHAPTER FORTY-THREE

3rd November, 24 Brownsfield Close, 6.45 a.m.

It was just before dawn when Lorraine's car pulled up outside number 26. Grace watched her get out and knock on Suzie's door. She met the two women on the doorstep, wearing her waterproof coat and holding a bulky backpack.

'What have you got in there, the Crown Jewels?' Lorraine quipped as she lifted the backpack into the boot. Suzie and Grace briefly exchanged looks as Lorraine chatted on. 'Change of plan,' she said as the three women climbed into the car. 'We've had a message that came in overnight. Some girl says she thinks she might have seen Billy out over Storey's Field way, so we thought we'd start there this morning. I've let the police know and the rest of the volunteers are meeting us there.'

She glanced across at Grace as they drove away from Brownsfield Close.

'Fingers crossed, eh?'

CHAPTER FORTY-FOUR

It was as the sky began to lighten and the last of the candles had flickered and died that Billy realized that the figures were slipping away. Some gradually became more faint and one by one faded to nothing. Others hugged their loved ones and waved, turned and walked away, slipping into gravestones or disappearing behind the trees. A slight breeze rustled the treetops and a fine drizzle began to fall. A greyness descended on the graveyard. It suddenly felt very empty and cold.

The old man emerged from between the yews. He walked slowly towards Billy. Steady and purposeful. Tears in his eyes and a smile on his face.

'That's a night to remember, eh?'

'I can't quite believe it,' said Billy. 'It's like a dream. So many people . . . and now it's as if they were never here.'

'But they'll be back. All Souls' Night next year. I tell you, when you love someone that much you'll wait a year to see them again.' The old man stared out at the graveyard as if trying to fix the night in his mind. 'You've seen, lad, the joy of seeing someone you've missed with all your bones, haven't you?' He looked sideways at Billy. 'Come on, let's clear up'. The old man turned to pick up the jam jars holding the spent candles.

Billy helped him collect them. They moved between the headstones quietly, each one lost in separate thoughts, the rustling of the trees overhead and the chink of the glass the only sounds.

Until they heard a distant dog bark. And another.

Then a faint shout.

'What's that?' asked Billy.

He walked to the edge of the graveyard, to where the pillbox stood, between the trees and the field beyond. The old man followed. They peered into the low mist that covered the field. There was another shout, followed by more.

'Is that someone calling my name?' asked Billy.
'I don't think it's just one person, lad,' said the old man.

Through the greyness a line of shadowy figures began to emerge in a neat line.

As they came nearer Billy could make out individual people. Some uniformed police, loads of strangers, Izzie, the tall bloke who he'd seen in the graveyard the day before and . . .

'Mum! My mum is there!' Billy took a step into the field. 'Mum!' he called.

He stumbled forward, towards the line of people, staggering on the uneven ground.

'Mum!' Billy called again.

Grace McKenna broke from the line of the search party and ran unsteadily in Billy's direction, her arms wide open to engulf him as he reached her.

'My boy. My Billy!' He buried his head in the warmth of her coat, breathing her in. 'I see you. I hear you. I've got you. My wonderful, *wonderful* boy.'

Billy took a step back and took in his mother's face. She beamed a wide smile that lit her face. His heart leapt – he remembered that smile. It had been so long since he'd seen it!

As they hugged, Billy noticed the old man stumbling on further towards the line of people.

'Come and meet my mum . . .' Billy called.

But the old man's eyes were fixed on that tall figure in
the scarf.

'Aye. In a minute, lad,' he said, his voice cracking
with emotion . . .

'But first I have to say hello to my son . . .'

THE END

ACKNOWLEDGMENTS

I have had so much help in making this book.

I gained so much insight into the plight of those suffering from domestic abuse and the professionals that support them from Amanda Warburton of Cambridge & Peterborough Domestic Abuse & Sexual Violence Partnership. The work that Amanda and her colleagues undertake is humbling and I am especially grateful that she found the time to share her experiences with me and to give feedback on drafts of this novel.

Retired policeman John Cox was so helpful in explaining how the police service really works (beyond my assumptions formed from binging too many TV crime dramas). He patiently explained police work, from shift patterns to the missing persons report process, and his knowledge has been invaluable.

I owe a huge debt of gratitude to both Amanda and John. Any alterations to the information they gave me are to assist the narrative and are not a reflection on their expertise. Hannah Webb and Ray Christofieds – thank you for guiding me to these specialists.

It has been lovely to work for Neil Dunnicliffe at Pavilion Books, along with editors Hattie Grylls and Martha Owen, and to have their enthusiastic support for this project. I have been nurtured through every step of the writing and editing of *The Hideaway* by the remarkable Alice Corrie, whose attention to detail and vision is breath-taking. Ness Wood, as always, has designed this book with customary flair. Thank you, all.

This book was inspired by the poem, 'All Souls' Night' by Frances Cornford. I am grateful to Enitharmon Press (www.enitharmon.co.uk) for their permission to reproduce this poem. You can enjoy more of Cornford's poems in this book: https://enitharmon.co.uk/product/selected-poems/.

As for every reader of this book, the year in which this story has been developed has been a challenging one. Vicci, Lucy, Lauren and Shelley – thank you for your extra kindness during this time.

Mila, you are a daily inspiration. Dave, your calm, steady and constant belief in this project has been the spell that has held me up and kept me going.

To all of you I offer my most heartfelt thanks.

Pam Smy, Cambridge, UK, September 2021

Pam Smy

Pam Smy is a Senior Lecturer Practitioner in Illustration on the MA Children's Book Illustration at Cambridge School of Art. She combines her teaching career with writing and illustrating.

She studied on the MA herself, graduating with the first cohort in 2004. Since then she has worked with a range of UK publishers including The Folio Society, Penguin Random House and David Fickling Books. She was short-listed for the CILIP Kate Greenaway Prize in 2018 for her first novel, *Thornhill*. *The Hideaway* is her first novel for Pavilion Children's Books.

Pam lives in Cambridge with her husband, author-illustrator Dave Shelton, and her child Mila. Most early mornings you'll see her walking her dog, Barney, along All Souls' Lane into the graveyard, past Frances Cornford's poem, the hidden pillbox and around the field beyond. When she isn't walking the dog, teaching and illustrating, Pam loves watching crime dramas and movies, drawing in sketchbooks, reading novels, comics and picture books.

OTHER BOOKS

Lob
written by Linda Newbery
illustrated by Pam Smy

The Brockenspectre
written by Linda Newbery
illustrated by Pam Smy

The Ghost of Thomas Kempe
written by Penelope Lively
illustrated by Pam Smy

The Ransom of Dond
written by Siobhan Dowd
illustrated by Pam Smy

Thornhill
written and illustrated by Pam Smy